PLAN #1

"We'll go on Saturday!" Annie said, excited.

"Rain or shine," David said.

"Nine-thirty," Annie said.

"Don't you be late!" Belinda teased.

"I won't be!"

"I'll pack the sandwiches," David said.

"One thing we have to figure out is how to get inside the cabin," Annie said. "It's padlocked."

"I can get in, but that's breaking in, isn't it?" David asked.

"It's on our own property and it's a good deed!" Annie said.

"I'm a little scared," Belinda said. "Are you?"

"Of course, kidnapping a dog, wow! We'd better make careful plans," David said.

"Kidnapping?" Annie said. "It's rescuing!"

When they left the rock pile that afternoon, everybody knew what they had to do. . . .

Bantam Skylark Books of related interest
Ask your bookseller for the books you have missed

ANNIE

AND THE

ANIMALS

BARBARA
BEASLEY
MURPHY

A BANTAM SKYLARK BOOK®
NEW YORK • TORONTO • LONDON • SYDNEY • AUCKLAND

RL 4, 008–012

ANNIE AND THE ANIMALS
A Bantam Skylark Book / September 1989
Bantam reissue / December 1991

ISBN 0-553-15749-3

Published simultaneously in the United States and Canada

*Bantam Books are published by Bantam Books, a division of Bantam
Doubleday Dell Publishing Group, Inc. Its trademark, consisting of the
words "Bantam Books" and the portrayal of a rooster, is Registered in U.S.
Patent and Trademark Office and in other countries. Marca Registrada.
Bantam Books, 666 Fifth Avenue, New York, New York 10103.*

PRINTED IN THE UNITED STATES OF AMERICA

OPM   0 9 8 7 6 5 4 3

For *Henryetta Kurtz Beasley*

. . . who recited "Curfew Shall Not Ring Tonight,"
"Young Thomas Jones," and "Casey at the Bat"
at the drop of a hat.

. . . who walked me on her feet
and brought me peanut butter to chomp in bed
when I couldn't sleep.

. . . who petted turtles on their wee heads
and sang "Pretty Redwing" in the kitchen
and shamelessly giggled at Herve Neille
singing *Aida* in the opera at the Cincy Zoo.

. . . who found everything for me!

. . . who always kneels to say her prayers to God,
who rises with the sunshine and
really sees the world without an enemy.

I'd like to salute her with seventy-six trombones
and a big parade,
but I think she'll be just as happy with *Annie,*
which is dedicated, with a grateful and
shamelessly boastful heart, to *her.*

ONE

Annie ran through her backyard, over the pretty rock wall between houses, and down the drive to woodsy Wellington Road.

She was racing to see Fritz, her favorite dog, the best dog, but a miserably unlucky dog! He lived across the road with a totally bad person. When Annie thought of the woman, she shivered. Mrs. Bardan did not deserve a dog like Fritz, nor any other dog.

Annie stopped at the edge of the road and stared at Mrs. Bardan's house, which was on a rise. She curled her hands tight in her warm mittens and peered up at the squat, mud-colored place. Its roof was droopy; its windows were draped and dark. No one who needed to know if Mrs. Bardan was there could tell. It was a grouch house with nothing stirring.

"Aha!" Annie said, even so. To see Fritz she had had to become a detective.

Where was "Old Snootface," "Old Beagle Ears," "Old Crab Mouth"? Annie wondered, going through her list of names for Mrs. Bardan. There was silence on the little hill.

Annie jiggled on the side of the road, trying to keep warm as she watched.

The leafless trees were still frozen. She pictured tiny baby leaves folded inside the hard buds of the trees, folded tight like origami doves. In December her fifth-grade class had made peace doves and sent them to Russian children in Moscow. Moscow was even colder than Syracuse, New York, where everybody was longing for spring. Today was the twenty-first of March, but Annie was dreaming of something more wonderful than the coming of spring. She was dreaming of freeing Fritz.

A shiny Mercedes swished by. A UPS truck. The phone company van.

"Where are you, witch?" she whispered, about to edge forward.

From down the street Annie heard kids giggling. The sound made her smile, and she felt a little braver. She walked across the road, her eyes down to give the appearance that she was concentrating on her feet and the new sneakers she was wearing.

Mrs. Bardan's garage was a separate wood building to the left of the house. The garage doors opened toward the house so Annie could not see if Mrs. Barden's car was inside or not.

There was a high dog cage by the side of the garage nearest the street. That was where Fritz lived. The cage was almost as tall as Annie's dad, who wasn't a shrimp. Annie now walked up the driveway toward the cage. She cringed as the gravel made crunching noises under her feet.

Let's see . . . if I see her, I'll say I was taking a shortcut to Belinda's. Or I'll say Mom sent me on an errand. Or maybe that I saw an accident and I'm running for Dr. Whitacre.

She reached the cage. "Ohhh, Fritz!" she breathed, happy to see the black German shepherd at last. But she was not happy about the way he looked.

"Poor dog!" she whispered. He lay in the corner like a pile of rags. His eyes were closed. Annie was sure that just since yesterday, he had shrunk. "Fritz?" she said, a bit louder.

He did not raise his head, nor move an ear, nor open his eyes. Annie was a little afraid he was dying.

But then his tail wagged, just slightly.

"Whew, oh good!" He was trembling, too. She could see that. "Come here. Come here!" Annie said gently.

Now she always had to coax him. He never smiled. She tapped the cage. "Come on, you can do it."

She glanced back at the silent house, and her heart thumped. She couldn't see anything, but she could feel somebody watching her. Could Mrs. Bardan make herself invisible?

Annie stuck her mittened hand into her pocket and fished out two flabby pieces of bacon. She had saved them from breakfast for Fritz.

She poked the bacon through the mesh. Fritz looked up, stuck out his long nose and sniffed. *Bacon*—it always worked! Magically, his half-crippled back end rose. He was standing. She wanted to cheer. But no! he was sinking. *No!* Coming over—yes! His black face was determined, but she noticed how dry his coat was.

The year before, Fritz had been injured by a speeding car. Hit and run. Until that awful day, he had patrolled Shawnee Park Neighborhood like a friendly policeman. All the kids loved him. Annie had known Fritz since she was born ten years ago and thought of him as *her* dog. They played in her yard and sometimes in the house, where they had made up a wild hide-and-seek game. He also liked to chase balls up and down her stairs, eat popcorn, and watch TV sometimes. As she grew up, they had explored the Syracuse Country Club nearby, playing all over the golf course in the wintertime. She gave him all the love and cuddles he received because Mrs. Bardan was colder than a crab's nose and never petted her dog.

Ever since Fritz was injured, Mrs. Bardan had kept him in the cage all the time. When anybody asked, she said she was just waiting for him to die.

Over and over Annie had begged Mrs. Bardan to let her take Fritz for walks on a leash. She would exercise him, she promised, would take the best care of him, would not let him get overtired. But the woman refused, sometimes even slamming the door in Annie's face. Mrs. Bardan didn't know enough not to treat an animal like a *thing,* Annie thought.

It was just like the pet store near the grocery store. The owner raised feeder mice to drop alive into the hungry jaws of snakes. Annie knew there were plenty of dead meats a person could feed a reptile, and she had spoken to the man in the store about it. He had laughed. So every time she had a chance, she would buy the poor little mice with some of her allowance and free them on the golf course. Annie herself ate no red meat, only chicken and certain fish. Never the poor lobsters she saw in tanks at stores and restaurants. Her views on animals had led to book reports on Jane Goodall, Albert Schweitzer, and *The Lion, The Witch and The Wardrobe,* her favorite novel. Her views on poor Fritz and the miserable treatment he was getting had led to wild thoughts. Now they had turned into big plans. Fritz took the bacon from her hand and gobbled it up. Annie cooed at him and petted his head through the wire mesh. He whimpered.

When he sank to the ground right there, she knelt down by the fence and continued to stroke and talk to him.

A nasty voice cut across the gentle whisper of her breath. "What are you doing here again?"

Annie spun around and fell on her bottom, then hurried to get up before Mrs. Bardan got there. She was marching across the yard hands on hips, wearing a maroon coat. It matched the poison-colored lipstick on her mouth, thought Annie. She hadn't heard the door; the old witch must have sneaked it open.

"I wasn't doing anything, Mrs. Bardan," she said as politely as she could over her angry feelings. "I was just passing through to Belinda's back there and on the way, said hello to your very nice dog." She pointed nervously to the house beyond the garage. "Honest, I was. Belinda has rabbits."

Annie was blubbering excuses because Mrs. Bardan looked so furious. Annie began backing toward her friend's house. If she turned her back, Mrs. Bardan might pounce on her.

Mrs. Bardan came up to her. Annie froze. She could feel her mouth twitch, which it did when she was scared.

"You like that dog?" Mrs. Bardan asked.

"Well, uh—yes, quite a lot. I've known him all my life. It was nice when he ran loose in the neighborhood. My mom thought so, too. She said it made the place safer for kids and—"

"Well, I don't. He's a lot of trouble now. Doesn't bark anymore and protect me. Did you ever notice that? He just whines all the time. I wish he were dead!"

Annie gasped. Mrs. Bardan, at the cage, pulled the stick out of the hasp on Fritz's lock and went inside to open a large can with a plastic lid. She dumped dry dog food into a bowl. Fritz shrunk from her as if he were afraid.

"Confounded fool! You've knocked your water over again." She leaned over and scooped up the grungy bowl, then hurried with it back into the house. Annie's eyes filled with tears, and she turned and ran to the yard behind Mrs. Bardan's. She crouched near Belinda's caged rabbits, her heart fluttering like a bird's. She listened for the woman to come back so she would be sure Fritz got his water. The dog whined; he knew she was still close. Annie felt desperate and angry. She couldn't understand Mrs. Bardan.

"Confounded fool yourself!" She stomped the frozen ground with her heel. "Don't worry, Fritzy, it won't be long. I promise."

Shivering, she ran across the lawn and knocked at Belinda's back door.

Two

☆

After school the very next day, Annie was in the Little Eagle buying pet food. The high shelves stocked full loomed over her while she studied that week's prices to get the best buys. All those cans, bright as flags. All the names—Alpo, Ken-L Ration, Kal-Kan, Canine Choice, Victory, Puppy Chow, Bow Wow! Burger Boy, King's Dog, Cadillac, Doggy Delight, Little Eagle's House Brand for Happy Dogs. One of the cans said right on it: *100 percent horsemeat.*

Annie screwed up her face. How could any human know which of these canned foods tasted good to a dog? All the TV ads showed dogs licking their bowls, but she knew better. She knew they starved the dogs about a week to get them to do that on cue.

The thought of the dogs eating horsemeat was making her queasy. She grabbed three of the cheapest cans off the shelves and hurried to the checkout counter. For weeks now she had been storing cans on the closet shelf behind her windbreaker, riding jacket, and hat. The balled-up clothes hid all the cans. Buying them knocked a hole in the big allowance she got from her dad each week. He was the Foam Rubber King of Syracuse—the sign over his shiny, clean store downtown said so. He could afford to give her a big allowance, thank goodness! But he was allergic to cats, rabbits, dogs, and guinea pigs—that was his one drawback. So the food wasn't for a pet of their own. Annie was the only one who knew she was going to need that dog food. No one else was in on it yet.

She had just given herself a name. She was calling herself the Animal Rescuer of Syracuse, New York, although she hadn't rescued any animals yet, and people still knew her as plain Annie Oberwager.

She knew, though, that a life's work didn't begin overnight. Think of Jane Goodall! It took planning, study, time to get ready. Buying the food was only part of her preparation. She wasn't going to wait until she grew up before she got started, either. Mozart wrote music at six; Dwight Gooden probably threw a fastball at five.

She laid out a dollar and some change on the white counter beside the cans and a box of animal crackers. She didn't eat these herself, but she had discovered some dogs liked them and wouldn't eat the regular biscuits that were shaped into bones and made for dogs. Fritz didn't like either kind much, but some dogs were very pleased to get them. One was Trapper, a beagle with the fastest mouth in town. She could catch any kind of cracker in the air as it was tossed. Since Trapper was on the chubby side, Annie tried not to overdo feeding her animal crackers. As Annie waited for the lady ahead of her to buy two cartloads of groceries, she smoothed her rumpled hair. The feel of it reminded her she needed a haircut, which reminded her that her mother wanted her to get one Saturday. That reminded her of how hard it was to fool her mother. *And* how much harder it might be to really pull off her plans. She wrinkled her nose, then rubbed that smooth, too.

When the cashier looked at her finally, he squeezed his eyes into slits and spoke through his nose. "You're always buying pet food," he said as though she were stealing.

She shook her head. "Not me! Maybe you've mixed me up with my sister . . . Gloria." Annie made her up on the spot. She might need an alibi later. "I'm doing it for her while she's got the chicken pox."

The skinny man frowned. He was holding on to a can, but he didn't move it across the price register light. He was giving her the hives.

"She looks just like you," he said.

"Well—I can't help that. . . ." She looked dumbly back at him, and so at last he rang up all her purchases and put them in a brown paper bag. She lifted it up and zipped it inside her jacket, then hurried out the door. She could handle the cashier. He seemed like a whiner, that was all.

The March wind shoved her down the street. Her red hair blew in front of her face. The trees along the sidewalk shivered in the blast of wind. She passed her brick school. In the empty lot next to it, a bunch of kids she knew were playing football. A shaggy dog with spots sprang away from the crowd of players and bounded over to her. He was wagging his tail so hard, his body rolled with it.

"Hi, Monster." She unzipped her jacket, reached into the bag, and took out the box of animal crackers. Quickly she opened it and tossed him a cracker. While busy with this, she peered at the group of kids to see who was there. She had a kind of hope in her heart. One that she couldn't think about too much or it would drive her nuts.

David Bernstein *was* there, heaving a football in a beautiful arc across the field. With arms still up he saw her and waved.

"Annie, come play tackle."

Her face flushed hot. "I wish I could, sorry I can't!" she cried, rushing off. *He always asks me. Sometime I've got to get up the nerve to say yes. It would be so much fun.* She giggled. *I like him,* she thought, amazed at the idea. Thrilled. Proud. *Scared.*

She crossed the street when it was clear both ways and ran down the hill into Shawnee Park Neighborhood where she lived. The huge houses were half a century old, and the trees had trunks fat enough to hide behind. Many years before, the neighborhood had been an orchard, her mother once told her. In spring, hundreds of ancient apple trees bloomed pink and white in every yard, a beautiful sight. Annie knew every backyard, every hill and tree, as well as all the animals. She even knew where Mohawk arrowheads could be found. Shawnee Park had a history that went back hundreds of years.

As she rushed home, she thought, *If I do decide to have a boyfriend, I will not be a mushy person.* That's what had happened to two of her friends when they got boyfriends. They talked about them all the time! And they stopped doing anything fun.

Dr. Whitacre drove by in his car and waved at her. She smiled and waved back and ran the rest of the way home. Her three-story house was English-style white stucco with two little windows on either side of the curved front door. It had a high-pointed roof. She pushed open the unlocked door and ran up the red-carpeted stairs to put everything away in her room before her mother came home from the foam-rubber store downtown. Josefina Gomez was putting her coat on at the closet before leaving to catch the bus. On Fridays she cleaned.

She called up to Annie after she flew by. "Can we go over the vocabulary one time before I go?"

Annie threw the stuff into the closet and ran down again. "Hi, Josie!" She gave Josefina a hug, and they stood at the door together while Josefina pulled some pieces of paper out of her pocket. She wrinkled up her face and read the word written on the first little piece of paper.

"Sunday," she said.

Annie beamed at her. "Sunday. Terrific."

"This one I got trouble with," Josefina said.

"Weekend. See, it's two words bunched up in one word."

"Oh. . . I see it now," Josefina said. "This is baby stuff. You ashamed of me?" Josie asked, cocking her head and looking at Annie sadly. Josefina had been a migrant worker's child; she was part Mexican and part something else, she said. She didn't know what because she had never known her mother. She was tall and pretty, with tan skin and smooth dark hair.

"How can you say that, Josie? I'm the one who wanted you to learn to read."

Josefina smiled. She had signed up for tutoring at the library only a month ago. Everybody in her family had coaxed her, to help her over the terrible shyness of being a grown-up and unable to read even one word in English.

"Two of my little kids are reading; they're just first and second graders. On Sunday they're joining me and my older kids in our singing group, God's Songbirds," Josefina told Annie.

"I love your singing group," Annie said, remembering a concert at Josefina's church.

They finished the collection of ten words. Then Josefina tucked the little packet safely inside her pocket again and said, "Annie, you call Belinda Shoof. She's been ringing the phone every ten minutes here. If I didn't get the house clean, it's because of that phone."

"I bet you were blabbing to Eddie," Annie said, giggling. Eddie was Josefina's boyfriend.

"Shame on you!" Josie said, suddenly looking taller as she marched through the door. "Don't you be fresh now with your elders!"

Josie was like two people, a helpless child and an imperious queen. She would shift back and forth from one to the other. Annie closed the door behind her and ran to the kitchen phone, which was ringing now.

THREE

☆

When she picked up the receiver, Annie said, "How are the rabbits, Belinda?"

"How'd you know it was *me*?" Belinda screeched.

"X-ray vision," Annie said. "How are they?"

"Oh, they're fine!" Belinda giggled. "The baby isn't nursing anymore, and now she's eating alfalfa."

"I saw her Thursday, she's so cute."

"Mmm," said Belinda.

"Too bad the other one had to die."

"Yeah. Aww . . ."

There was silence on the line. Then Belinda said, "But he was weak, a runt, and if he hadn't died, he might have been sick his whole life."

"I know it." Annie yanked at her socks. "I just saw David playing ball. Same old runny nose. You like him?"

"David Bernstein? No."

"I don't either," Annie said, crossing her fingers. "But in music he told me that he's got a red Irish setter puppy. Brand new! Only weeks old!"

"Wow! I didn't know that!"

15

"Want to go see it?"

"Sure. Why don't you come over first thing in the morning?"

"Okay," Annie said. "Right after breakfast."

As soon as she had hung up, Annie ran upstairs to straighten the things in her closet. But before she could get the dog food arranged, the front door opened. Her parents were both home from work—early. "Annie!" she heard them call.

"Be there in a minute!" she grumbled, climbing up on a desk chair because a can had fallen off the shelf and clunked her on the head.

"What are you doing up there?" Mrs. Oberwager asked, sticking her head around Annie's half-closed door. She brushed a lock of hair out of her eyes. "Hiding my birthday present?"

"Mom! It's *not* your birthday. It's just . . . Josie, the phone, you came home early . . ." Annie jumped down and shoved the closet door, but it didn't close because of the chair in the way. She ran to her mother and gave her a hug.

"This is all I wanted!" her mom said, hugging her back. They plopped down on the bed, which was near the door, and had a cuddle. It made Annie take a nice, deep breath to be so close to her mom. She relaxed. Her mother still had her coat on, and it smelled like the cold Syracuse air. Her pink nose felt like an ice chip against Annie's cheek. Then her dad came up to her room. He was six foot four and good looking. When he saw them, he decided to plop on *both* of them, smothering them with his big body and scratchy tweed jacket.

"What is this?" Annie asked, giggling. "Perverts!"

"It's just the Oberwager zoo!" her dad yelled, tickling Annie.

She petted his head. "Animals aren't bald," she teased. Mr. Oberwager had a shiny bald head, but he could take a tease.

"You are *so* rude!" he said, giving her curly hair a yank and laughing.

"Ow!"

Before Annie could get the two of them out of there, they had a lot of silly fun. All she could think of, though, was that one of them was going to walk over and peer into the closet. She wasn't positive that her mom hadn't already seen the stuff on the shelf. As soon as they were gone, Annie put the clothes back in place to hide the canned pet food.

It was the "crack of noon" when Annie got up the next morning—that was what her mother called eleven A.M. It was too late for the haircutter's, thank goodness! Annie thought.

Annie quickly dressed and ate breakfast. Then she put on her kelly green jacket and went over to Belinda's. She took the long way round, skipping a visit to Fritz. She knew she needed to be clever about that. Otherwise, her plans could be blown.

The misty day had looked warm from inside the house, but it was definitely chilly outside. Annie had dressed for it, though, and was whistling as she strolled up Belinda's walk.

Before Annie got all the way up to it, Belinda opened the door to her house. "Hi, Oberwager!" "Hi, Shoof!" Annie replied. They both had funny names.

Belinda was wearing a fuzzy, orange-red cardigan sweater over a blouse. It went with her fuzzy yellow hair and her fuzzy eyelashes. She had toast crumbs on the sweater, which Annie pointed out to her right away.

Belinda picked one off and ate it, fuzz and all. "Cinnamon. Want some?"

Annie made a face.

"Wait a sec, I'll be out." Belinda put on a heavy blue jacket over the sweater and shouted good-bye to her family. Then she and Annie started off toward David's house.

A police car drove by and then an ambulance. "I'm interested in what goes on around here. Maybe we should follow them," Belinda said.

The ambulance turned a corner. "I only like to follow fire engines," Annie said. "If you follow an ambulance, nobody ever tells you what's the matter. It just gets up your curiosity."

When they neared the Bernstein house, a boxy place with several levels, Belinda whispered, "Their house is a disaster."

"It's just modern architecture."

"Mommy says it spoils the whole neighborhood," Belinda said.

"You're crazy, Belinda. I'm dying to see inside it."

Belinda laughed, "Me too! Do we ring the bell?"

"Let's just go around back and see if the dog's there. David will come out if he sees us."

They walked up the driveway. Behind the house was a fenced-in pool. Belinda's eyes lit up at the sight of it. "I forgot. I do like him!"

Annie gave her a poke. The dog wasn't in the doghouse or anywhere in the yard. "Hey, David!" Annie called.

No answer.

"You have to ring the doorbell, Annie!"

"You're right. You do it, okay?"

"Not me. You!" Belinda said.

"Hey!" The voice had come from the back of the garden.

"That's David!" Annie exclaimed, embarrassed at the delight in her own voice.

They turned to see David halfway up a rocky hill in the far corner of the lot. When they got there, he was peeking out of a hole between two giant boulders.

"Whoa! You got mountains as well as a swimming pool!" Belinda exclaimed.

Annie blushed.

"When they dug the hole for the basement of our house, the workmen piled all the stuff here. It's just a rock pile filled in with dirt and plants," David said, wiping his freckled nose on his sleeve.

Annie noticed the gray sweatshirt he wore every day of the year to class. When it was cold he would wear eighteen layers of sweaters under it. Today was not freezing, so he didn't have that bunchy, padded look.

"I think you should come over here. I hear something," he said.

"Where's the puppy?" Annie asked, putting her knee on a rock and pulling herself up. Belinda was behind her. Then Annie got to the place where she could squeeze herself between two big boulders. David was putting one ear against a narrow space between two other rocks. His straight brown hair was sticking to the back of his neck.

"Hear it?" he whispered.

Annie and Belinda listened. In a moment there came a tiny cry. David put his finger up, but didn't say anything.

Again they heard the sound. "Where's it coming from?" Annie whispered.

Belinda pointed up. David got to his feet and started climbing to the top of the rock pile. Dirt, sticks, and brown leaves jostled loose by his boots came down in little shower. Annie had to shut her eyes and turn her head to keep it out of her face.

"Hey, I see two eyes and paws . . . and . . . it's a kitten!" he shouted.

Annie scrambled the rest of the way up. "Let me see it!"

David was holding up a filthy white kitten.

"It's so skinny!" Belinda said, jumping around to the other side of David.

"Poor thing!" Annie said, her heart pounding. She reached out and David placed the frail animal in her hands. "Oooh." It pressed against her wool jacket. Carefully holding the kitten, she climbed down the rock pile as David and Belinda followed.

Then David walked into the scraggly woods near the rocks. "Maybe its mother's here." But he came back shaking his head.

Belinda was stroking the cat in Annie's arms. "It's so hungry!" she said when the kitten nibbled her finger. The kitten meowed.

"Oh, boy, what are we going to do with it?" David said.

"Can't we take it inside and feed her a little milk?" Annie asked.

David moaned. "Not here. My folks hate cats and Rebel will kill her."

"Cute name!" Belinda said about the puppy. He blushed.

"You take her, Belinda," Annie said.

Belinda sighed and shook her head. "No more animals. We've got the rabbits. Mommy's put her foot down."

"Well," Annie said, "my dad's allergic to cats, asthmatic and—"

"No problem! We'll call the animal shelter!" David said.

"What, are you crazy!" Annie yelled. David stepped back, hurt.

"I'm sorry. I thought you knew. They gas them. They get a hundred kittens a month and can't find homes for ten. They have to gas them."

David and Belinda moaned. The kitten whined.

"I've got an idea," Annie said. "David, can I use your phone?"

"Sure," David said. "Come on."

They went inside David's house. Belinda's and Annie's eyes widened as they walked into the Bernstein kitchen, which was large, shiny, and modern. Annie called Josefina at her home. You could have heard her *no* all the way to Canada.

"I thought you were my friend," Annie whined, exasperated. She tried to explain once more. Josefina cut her off before she got to the bony ribs part again. She said she was going to the foot doctor's and then to the library. "To get me some Shakespeare." Of course she was joking about that.

Annie covered the receiver with her hand and whispered, "No time for animals. Period." She said good-bye and hung up.

Mrs. Bernstein gave them chocolate cookies, then shooed them and the cat out of her squeaky-clean kitchen. Annie could feel the kitten's bones poking into her fingers and its heartbeat tapping gently, helplessly against her skin. Annie felt nervous. The kitten's fur was so dirty. He or she might be full of fleas and mites. Annie was wishing David or Belinda wanted to hold it, but neither of them offered and she didn't ask. How could she be an animal rescuer if she was afraid of fleas and mites?

Maybe this was a test that had fallen out of heaven into her hands. To train her for the big move ahead.

"What're you thinking about?" David asked, looking into her eyes with his very nice gray ones.

She looked back at him and just smiled.

"Well. What'll we name it?" Belinda said.

"You'll take it, won't you, Annie?" David said. "We'll help you."

"Well . . . I guess so," Annie said, not sure what to do. Maybe she could take it home for a few days, just until they found the kitten a permanent home.

"What'll we name it?" Belinda asked.

"Wow, Belinda, you move fast," David said. "We haven't got it a permanent home yet."

"If it doesn't have a name, David, it'll be bad for its confidence," Belinda said flatly.

Annie checked to see if the cat was male or female. It was female.

"April. I'm calling her April," Annie said as they drifted down the driveway toward the street. Suddenly she realized why she and Belinda had gone to David's house. "You never showed us your dog!"

"Oh, sorry. Next time, okay?"

Annie began to worry about taking the kitten home. *I can't tell my mom I'm doing this, and Mom likes only the truth.* She would have to hide the kitten in her attic.

An ambulance with flashing lights roared by them on the narrow street. It followed the curve and disappeared.

"Is that the one we saw earlier?" Belinda asked, touching Annie's arm.

"Looks the same."

"Brr!" Belinda said, holding on now.

As they hurried toward the Oberwagers' house on Valley Road, they explained to David about the police car and ambulance they had seen earlier. They told him they hated it when they couldn't find out why an ambulance or a police car stopped at a house.

"It's against the law for the attendants to tell you. It's an invasion of privacy if they do," David explained.

They had reached the rock wall between the neighbors' and Annie's back yards. As they were about to jump over, Belinda pointed out the snow that clung to the inside of the rocks. "Snowpussies," she said. "Did you know that's what they're called?"

Annie and David giggled. They hadn't known that. The shivering kitten raised her little head and looked at Annie.

"What a cute little nose you've got!" Annie said. "And pretty soon you're going to be nice and warm in our attic."

The kids went around the back of the house to the side door.

FOUR

☆

"Shhh!" Annie said.

Just before she opened the side door, David stuck the little kitten under his sweatshirt. *Let him get the fleas!* Annie thought.

Everybody tiptoed in.

Annie led the way into the front hall, and they started up the stairs. When they turned at the landing, they saw Mrs. Oberwager coming down.

"Oops!" Belinda said.

Annie coughed. David's face turned red.

"What's this!" Annie's mother said, startled.

"Hi, Mom!" Annie said.

"What're you guys up to?" she said, laughing because they had all almost bumped into each other. She was wearing blue jeans, and her soft hair was tied back.

"We're . . . uh . . . I'm just taking them up to my room," Annie said.

"What for?" Mrs. Oberwager said, standing in the middle of the steps like an intersection cop.

Annie shrugged. "Oh, they want to see something . . . my Pictionary game. . . ."

David sniffed.

"And I've got to give David a tissue. He's got a cold. Belinda's got to go to the bathroom," Annie said as fast as the ideas came to her. David was wiggling.

"Well, okay. Guess I'll let you by, but you sure look like the cat that caught the mouse." Her eyes sparkled as she looked from face to face. "Nice to see you, Belinda. And David, isn't this your first time here? Have a good time!" She smiled, squeezed over to the side, and let them pass.

"Nice to see you, Mrs. Oberwager," Belinda said, starting to giggle.

Everybody pounded upstairs. At the top, Annie turned around and yelled down. "You going to work in the garden, Mom?"

"No, why?" she answered. "It's March."

"Just wondered. You've got your jeans on."

"I don't wear these in the garden," Mom said. Annie heard her go into the kitchen and hoped they hadn't made her mother suspicious.

Belinda and David dashed into Annie's room. Annie dived in after them. They all fell on the floor, hands over their mouths, trying not to laugh. But of course that didn't help. They couldn't stop laughing.

"I do have to go to the bathroom now," Belinda said and giggled. She jumped up and ran down the hall. David pulled the kitten out of his shirt. She started to yowl.

"Shhh!" Annie said. "Why didn't she cry when she was in your shirt?"

"I was holding her mouth. Put your radio on."

"You weren't!" she said, rolling over and reaching the radio on her nightstand. They played it loud.

"I was. But I had to."

"Suppose she had suffocated?"

"I knew what I was doing!"

"Oh, boy!" Annie said, glad that he did.

Belinda came back, and Annie got up from the floor where she had been sitting. "Ready? We have to take April upstairs to the attic."

"This is never going to work," Belinda said.

"Oh, shut up! Give it a try," David said.

Annie led the way to the third-floor door and up the stairs. They walked down a short hallway, and Annie opened the attic door. It was freezing cold inside.

"It's just like outside, brrr!" Belinda complained. "I thought you said she'd be warm in the attic, Annie."

"That cat's used to the temperature," David said.

He was really smart, Annie thought. She rummaged among some old newspapers. Then she opened a trunk and took out some beach towels and old sofa pillows. With all that they made a cozy nest in a ring of suitcases.

"It's really good to put the suitcases around like this because it's such a big room," David said. "This way the cat'll know where home is."

The kitten cowered in the corner of its nest and cried. The sound made Annie itchy. "We'd better get her something to eat," she said, wishing she had thought to buy cat food when she was stocking up at the store.

"Can we ask your mom for cookies and milk?" Belinda wanted to know.

"Terrific idea!" Annie said.

Down they went. Annie's mom was Mrs. Agreeable and said, "Anything you want, honey."

The cookies were in a pottery jar with a clown face on it. They took a quart of milk from the refrigerator. Minutes later they were on their way back up. David had snitched an ashtray from the living room as they went through. It would hold the milk.

When they placed the ashtray brimful of milk at her feet, April just looked at it.

David stuck his finger in it and brought it up to the kitten's mouth. She tasted it. "Mmm," said Belinda. "Good, huh?"

After some more coaxing, April lowered her little head, taking sweet little slurps of the milk. Belinda sighed with happiness. Drinking the milk had finally stopped the kitten's crying.

"She was making me crazy, too," Annie admitted.

April paused and looked up. It seemed as if she were seeing them for the first time. Her eyes were two little exclamation-point dots.

"She looks surprised!" David said rubbing the stubby cowlick on his head.

Annie smiled at him. "Doesn't she eat pretty?"

Belinda hugged herself. "She's saying thank you."

"I've seen the farmer's cows out at our farm. If you give them an ear of corn, they look at you so sweetly."

"April's a super-duper cat!" David said. He was beaming. "We'll put an ad in the morning announcements, and some kid'll take her."

"Or maybe a teacher. That'd be the safest," Annie said.

"Or a custodian. Mr. Wunderly. He loves animals. A lot of custodians do," Belinda said, as if nobody else could figure that out.

"What'll we do if *everybody* wants her?" Annie said.

But nobody did.

On Monday, Tuesday, and Wednesday, the principal announced the kitten needed a home. Lots of kids said they would like to help out, but nobody did. It made Annie mad. *What's the matter with the world?*

When nobody took April by Thursday, Annie was desperate. As they were walking home from school, she said to Belinda and David, "Hey, listen! I've got to do something. I think I've caught fleas from her, look!" She rolled down her yellow knee socks and showed them six big pink bumps.

"Oh! Gross!" Belinda said.

"It looks like chicken pox, think it could be that?" David asked.

Annie felt disgusted that David was talking about chicken pox. "I've *had* chicken pox!"

"Do they itch?" Belinda asked, more gently.

"Do they!" Annie moaned. She reached down and scratched.

"Don't scratch!" David said.

"Shut up! I have to, dummy!" she yelled.

He looked miserable.

"April's making such a mess upstairs, I can't clean it all up. She doesn't stay in the part of the attic we gave her. She goes all over it. I have to play my radio loud so my folks won't hear her cry. Sometimes I sleep up there. Last night Dad was sneezing and rubbing his eyes. I'm afraid he'll have an asthma attack." Annie scratched an itchy spot. "I love April, but . . ." Tears suddenly popped into her eyes, and she had to blink them back.

"Boy! And after what you told me, I don't want to put her in the animal shelter," David said. He sounded sad.

They crossed over into Shawnee Park Neighborhood. It was such a nice day they didn't need hats or mittens.

"We just can't put her there," Belinda said. "That'd be almost as terrible as what Mrs. Bardan is going to do to her dog."

Annie stopped in her tracks. "What? What is she going to do?"

"Mommy said that Mrs. Bardan's going to put Fritz

to sleep. He never healed after the accident, and there's some other reason I can't remember."

"No, she can't do that! He's still healthy and strong!" Annie looked at Belinda and felt afraid.

"Well, it's just what my mother heard. A friend of hers, Mrs. Keene, volunteers at the shelter. She told my mom that Mrs. Bardan called asking if they'd do it free."

"Ohh!" David made a face.

"Mrs. Keene told her she'd have to take the dog to her vet's."

"Her own dog!" David said, disgusted.

Belinda put her hand on Annie's shoulder. "I know you like him a lot."

"I love him." Annie's mind raced. If Mrs. Bardan was really planning this, the time for getting ready was up.

Can I trust them? she wondered.

A school bus roared past and stopped at the corner house. Two boys got out, and the bus, spewing filthy exhaust, zoomed on. The boys stopped in the yard to pet their black Labrador, who was welcoming them home.

Annie sighed as she, Belinda, and David walked by. "I have a secret."

Belinda and David stopped and turned. Belinda's blue eyes darkened. "What is it?" she asked in a special tone as if somehow she might have already guessed it.

"What?" David said slowly, looking from one to the other.

"I'd have to be sure you won't tell. . . ." Annie said, embarrassed to confess that she might doubt them just a little.

"Annie, I love secrets. You know I can keep them!" Belinda's eyes were glowing now. She crossed her heart.

David sneezed and used a tissue and then looked very seriously at Annie, too. "I think we should lay quarters on it. Then you'll know you can trust us."

"What do you mean?"

"My brother, Kenny, who's in high school, told me about it. Everybody in on the secret puts a quarter in the same safe place, a place everybody can get to. They tape their initials to the coins, and if anybody ever feels he wants to tell the secret, then he first has to mail the quarter with his own name on it to the guy who told the secret. Then he has to wait until the secret-teller lets him know he got the quarter and if it's okay now for the thing to be told!" David sneezed again and said, "Allergies."

Annie and Belinda were listening very carefully to what David was saying about secrets. They were near Mrs. Tuttle's house; she was the lady who taught piano.

"If the guy tells without mailing the quarter," David continued, "he'll never be able to have any children."

"That's really something!" Belinda said.

"Yeah!" Annie agreed.

They started on; Annie was quiet.

Belinda nudged her. "Well, I've got my quarter. Right here!" She patted her coat pocket.

"Me, too. And we can keep them in the rocky hill behind my house, okay? Got one, Annie?"

"A quarter?" She nodded yes. "But I have to think about it a little longer."

"Oh, come on!" Belinda begged.

"Yeah, Annie, we want to be in on it. Can't you trust us?" David said.

They had reached the corner where Annie would have to go her way and Belinda and David, theirs. Both of Annie's friends were staring at her.

"Annie!" Belinda coaxed, nudging her shoe against Annie's toe.

It was now or never. "Okay!" Annie shouted, feeling a sudden rush of happiness. It was the right thing to include her best friends, of course! "Let's go up to the rock pile and I'll tell."

"All *right*!" David said, socking her arm and making her heart go *thump*.

"And you can finally show us Rebel," Belinda yelled, getting on the other side of him. His face turned beet red.

"About time, too!" Annie said, laughing and socking him back a little.

David sneezed again.

"God bless you!" she said.

FIVE

☆

When they got to David's, he ran inside and brought out Scotch tape. By now Annie could hardly wait to tell. Little firecrackers of excitement were popping in her head. Up on the rocks David carefully ripped a slip of lined paper into even strips. They each wrote their initials on a strip, taped them over their quarters, and then buried them in a hole David dug in the dirt between the rocks. The earth was damp, soft and easy to push around. It smelled of spring.

"I think it's a good sign we're burying the coins where David was standing when he first heard the cat," Annie said.

"As long as the money's here, the secret's safe," David said. "Okay?"

Annie, who was bursting by now, told them her secret name, the Animal Rescuer of Syracuse. They didn't laugh at this, which gave her confidence to go further. She said she planned to rescue any mistreated, abused, or homeless animals that she came into contact with.

"Most of all I've wanted to save Fritz. And now,

after what you told me, Belinda, I have to. In a way, you know, he's really my dog. I've always loved him and looked out for him as much as Mrs. Bardan would let me."

"She's so mean!" Belinda said. "Witchy!"

"David Bernstein thinks you've got a great idea!" David said firmly. "Congratulations!" He shook Annie's hand. Afterward she dropped it to her ankles and scratched. The bites were itching like mad.

"I could tell you more things about Mrs. Bardan," Belinda said. "She lives behind me."

"Wait, let Annie finish," David said.

"I've been waiting until I got enough dog food to feed Fritz for a month before I took him away. Last count, I had thirty-two cans saved up."

"Wow!" David said as she explained where it was hidden.

"And this is the best part." Annie looked down, swallowed, and took a big breath. "The most important part of the secret is that I have a *place* to take Fritz. There will be plenty of room for April, too! But I need help getting there."

Belinda and David were nodding and said at the same time, "We'll help you!"

"You have to cross your hearts and swear you'll never tell, quarters or not, okay?"

They crossed their hearts and swore they would never tell. In the sunlit trees behind them, Annie could see the sparkle of the spring buds, now purple red. The glow shone around her friends. She leaned forward, so close that their hands nearly touched.

Belinda already knew that the Oberwagers owned a farm, but David didn't. Annie explained that her parents rented it out. "It's about two miles from here," Annie said. "And there's an abandoned old scout cabin on the property. It's totally empty, and nobody ever goes anywhere near it."

"That's amazing," Belinda said. "You never told me about the cabin."

"When can we go?" David said.

"Right away, we have to do it right away!" Belinda said.

"David! Oh, David!" Mrs. Bernstein was calling. His head jerked at the sudden sound of his mother's voice from the house.

"Time to practice," she called.

"Oh, nuts, my mother's always calling at the wrong—"

"We'll go Saturday!" Annie said, excited. It was about to come true. Her dream.

"Rain or shine," David said.

"Nine-thirty," Annie said.

"Don't you be late!" Belinda teased.

"I won't be!"

"I'll pack sandwiches, you carry the cat," David said.

"David!" His mother called again.

"I've got to go."

"We haven't seen your puppy!" Belinda moaned.

"I know, I know!" David said. "Sorry!"

"When I get my allowance Friday morning, I'll have money for cat food. April's eaten all the tuna in the house," Annie said.

"I can bring milk in a thermos," Belinda said. David stood up, ready to go.

"One thing, we have—"

"David, are you coming?" Mrs. Bernstein yelled once more.

"One thing we have to figure out is how to get inside the cabin," Annie said. "It's padlocked."

"And rusted, too, I bet. I can get in, but that's breaking in, isn't it?" His mother yelled again. This time she sounded really mad.

"It's on our own property and it's a good deed!" Annie said.

"I'm a little scared," Belinda said. "Are you?"

"David!" Mrs. Bernstein screamed.

"Of course, kidnapping a dog, wow! We'd better make careful plans," David said, ignoring his mother completely. He sat back down with them on the rocks.

"Kidnapping? It's rescuing!" Annie pointed out.

"Be right back, just wait a minute." David ran down and quickly talked to his mother, who was standing in the kitchen door. Then he raced back, and for five minutes more they made plans. When they left the rock pile that afternoon, everybody knew what to do.

SIX

"Over my dead body!" Josefina hollered, her face a tropical storm, her arms up over her head holding the wicker wastebasket, the howling kitten inside it.

Annie, just coming in the door, was stunned at the sight.

"Cats in the Oberwager house! I'm not going to put up with it," Josefina said. "Your mother and fa—"

"Josie, listen to me! Please!" Annie pleaded, reaching up with her hands to snatch the wastebasket Josefina was waving above her head in the front hall.

April scratched at the woven straw and for a second the tip of her white head, hair standing up, poked over the top. Josefina shouted she had discovered her in the attic, and she threatened to show her to Annie's parents when they came home. The clock in the hall said five-fifteen; they could be there in less than five minutes.

"Please, Josie!" Annie pleaded, unable to reach the wastebasket. "Don't tell, I'm begging you."

Josefina danced out of the way as Annie lunged again, slapping her knuckles into the wall. "Ouch!" she said miserably. "I'm warning you . . ."

"You're warning me? I've known your folks since before you were eating baby food, child. They allow no animals on these premises, and you know it. It's my duty to tell them you're not obeying the rules."

Maybe she couldn't read, but Josefina sure could talk. She had screeched the words at Annie as she moved toward the kitchen. Annie followed. Josefina put the wastebasket atop the refrigerator. The cat was peering over the basket rim.

"Get in there, you trespasser!" Josefina yelled, taking a frying pan lid off the counter next to the stove and clapping it over the wastebasket. *She has some reach,* Annie thought. She breathed in the rich smell of chicken steaming on the stove. It made her queasy.

"Josie!" she begged, nearly out of her mind. "Don't tell."

"Heaven help us! It's got fleas. Your mama's got a right to know what's in her house. How are you going to be better if I don't tell and if you're not punished for your sins? It's my duty, young lady, to not let you run wild like the other youngsters do in this fancy-pants neighborhood."

"Josie, please give me the cat. April's mine. I'll take her straight to Belinda's, I promise," Annie begged, her throat so tight she almost couldn't talk.

Josefina's long, spread-out fingers pressed firmly on the covered wastebasket; the cat was crying and making Annie feel so sad.

"If Belinda wanted the cat, she could have had it by now. There must be some reason you got it, and I expect it's because you don't have anybody else who will keep it because their mom and dad say the same thing your mom and dad do, and what *I* said when you asked *me* to take it." Josefina grabbed a gulp of air and continued pouring out the words like they were putting out a fire. "Only those other youngsters listen and you don't! That's what's naughty."

The gravel in the driveway crunched. There was the rumble of the garage door being pushed up. The garage was to the side of the house, and Annie's parents soon would come in the side door.

"I know, I'm sorry, but I do, cross my heart, have some place to take her. Tomorrow." Annie crossed her heart, which was thumping wildly. "If you don't tell . . . I'll help you more with your reading and I'll give you . . . twenty dollars. I promise, Josie, twenty dollars."

Annie knew it was a lot. She would have to take it out of her piggy bank.

"You haven't got no right to own a cat!" Josefina said thoughtfully, her brown eyes still sharp. "Twenty dollars? You think you can buy me off?"

"No," Annie said, looking at her hopefully, tears filling her eyes. "I'm just trying to save her life!" Annie clutched Josefina's other hand. It was soft and cool.

"If I take this money . . . it'll punish you for disobeying?"

"Yes. Yes, ma'am," Annie said, just like Josefina's own children did. Forgiveness and mercy began to shine in Josie's eyes.

"I *could* give it to the church," Josefina said. "But I can't take your money. It wouldn't be right. Here!" she said, bringing down the wastebasket. "Run it upstairs, honey. And you better find a home for it *soon!*"

"Oh, thank you, Josie!" Annie cried as the side door handle clicked as it was turned.

Just in the nick of time Josefina lowered the basket into Annie's waiting arms. As the door banged open, Annie ran out of the kitchen and through the house to the stairs. She raced the cat, with a hand on its bony little back, all the way up to the third floor and into the attic. She dumped her out of the wastebasket on to the clean-swept floor. It smelled like it had been washed! The wide planks of the attic floor looked dark and felt damp when Annie tested them with her fingers. The kitten scampered off to the side after Annie gave her a big kiss and set her down gently. There wasn't a sign of cat dirt anywhere.

Josefina's help was worth more than money! Annie kissed the kitten once more, checked her food and water, then closed the attic door. She hurried down the short hallway and down the stairs to the second floor. She closed the other door carefully behind her, pulled off her jacket and flung it into her bedroom. Then with her heart still fluttering, she hurried downstairs.

"Hi, Mom!" she said softly, seeing her mother at the hall table separating the junk mail from the letters. She was wearing a blue winter coat with a matching woolen scarf around the neck. It made her eyes look blue as the sea.

"Hi, honey!" she said, stopping what she was doing and leaning toward Annie to give her a kiss. She smelled like lily of the valley perfume, and her cheeks gleamed from the cold. "Look! Here's a letter from New Mexico! Rosie!"

Rosie was her mother's sister. The vet. The one Annie figured she got her talent with animals from.

Josefina and Mr. Oberwager came out of the kitchen. He was carrying his big camel-hair coat and went to the closet to hang it up. He turned to say hi to Annie. "Treat day," he said, handing her a small white paper bag. Josefina stared at Annie.

"See *you* next week!" Josefina said, her voice full of extra meanings. She went to the closet to get her coat and violet hat.

Annie felt her cheeks go hot. "Hi, Dad!" she said.

He seemed to be staring at her. He was always sensitive to her feelings, and Annie was aware of trying to hide them. She squeezed the top of the unopened paper bag. Her mother took her mail and went upstairs.

"And do as you should!" Josefina added as she buttoned her coat, making it all the harder for Annie to act as if nothing had happened.

Josefina pulled the front door open, and the chilly air blew in. "Good-bye, Mr. Oberwager!" she said. "Bye, Mrs. Oberwager!" she called up the stairs. She swept out, letting the door close softly behind her. Mr. Oberwager followed to see it was tight; he didn't like losing heat.

"What was that all about, huh?" He raised his eyebrows at Annie and gave her a boyish smile. His bald head was pink from the cold.

"Who knows?" Annie said, summoning all her innocence and wandering into the den to watch TV. She needed a snack. Needed to sit down. Wanted to look in the bag.

"Are you up for a game of Trivial Pursuit tonight, sweet face?" her dad asked, following. He gave her shoulder a friendly shove with his hand.

"I'm going to watch the news for social science!" she said, too quickly. *Slow down,* she told herself. "And then I have to study for a science report I'm going to write tomorrow. I'll be at the library all day!" She had to plan carefully for the next day.

Annie clicked on the TV, then opened the paper bag. She laughed at what was inside. It was a rubber stamp that said, "The Stupids Live!" referring to a book she and her father had read a thousand times.

"Isn't it great?" Mr. Oberwager said.

She loved it.

Mr. Oberwager settled with a happy groan into the leather chair; Annie curled up on the sofa. She listened with all her attention when the weatherman, whom her dad called Mr. Blow, came on and talked in his breathless voice. She dozed off when the commercial came on.

Mrs. Oberwager nudged Annie with a dinner tray. "We can eat in here tonight, but you'll have to wake up first." She put down a plateful of steaming hot food on the coffee table near Annie. The chicken, which had made her feel queasy only a little while ago, was covered with rich cream gravy and slivered almonds and surrounded by fresh green beans and mashed potatoes.

Annie sat up and swung her feet down. "Mmm," she said gratefully.

Everybody smiled at one another when they were all settled. It was the Oberwagers' favorite meal.

"And I got our deli cole slaw!" her dad said, pointing to a full container of it that he had set down next to Annie's plate. She sighed, feeling happy in all her bones.

"And I'll make us sundaes," Annie promised.

Everybody smiled again. The Oberwagers weren't dieters; no, they were eaters. Annie's father loved to brag about the food they could put on their table. Since he had been very poor when he was a boy, he couldn't get over having enough food for everybody and more besides. He was rich and glad of it! Sometimes it was embarrassing.

Later, after gobbling down the yummy food, Annie sat in front of the fire her father built in the living room fireplace. She stared at the twisting, crackling, popping flames. Her father dozed on the couch, his feet in smooth black socks, his round belly, which he insisted he was proud of, rising into the air with every snoring breath he took.

Mrs. Oberwager was upstairs reading *Beautiful Swimmers,* a book about crabs, she said. Nobody had felt like playing Trivial Pursuit. Annie sighed. The wiggling fire leaped at the brass mesh fireplace screen, trying to get out. Like Fritz! Annie was mesmerized, her heart now hopeful, then anxious.

She felt she couldn't tell her folks the truth. Hiding the animals was the only way she could think of to save them. But she felt so guilty.

It wasn't wrong to help the pets. Didn't she have the right, young as she was? But what if she, David, and Belinda didn't succeed? A tear rolled down her cheek, and she licked it off with her tongue. *Nuts!* she thought.

The fire flared high, its center a pair of eyes that peered sternly at Annie and then softened and disappeared, causing her to suddenly kiss her dad good night and hurry up to bed. She slipped into her mom's room on the way and waved good night. She didn't feel like kissing, but her mother pulled her into her arms for a hug. Annie could have stayed, but instead she broke away and went quietly to her room. She had a lot of things to gather for the rescue. Also, she wanted to get a good sleep so she would wake up with plenty of energy. Tomorrow she would save April and Fritz.

SEVEN

☆

On TV, Mr. Blow had predicted a fifty percent chance of snow. Thinking she could hear it falling, Annie woke up and jumped out of bed. She pressed her nose against the cold windowpane. The sky was as dark as old winter coats, and all the stars were hidden. It must have been the wind's huff in the juniper trees, she thought, because there wasn't any snow to be seen. If it did snow, their boot tracks could be followed all the way from Fritz's cage to the secret cabin.

But in the morning the wind had died and a strange quiet settled on the street. Annie stared out sleepily, dreaming of all they were going to do. Excited, she hugged herself and watched the white sky.

She went over her plans. First Belinda would call and ask her over so they could work on the report together all day. Annie would say they were going to the library together. Then Belinda would call David, who would get permission to go to her house. Then he'd call Belinda and she would get permission to go to his! After this was done, they would make their move.

Nine-thirty sharp at Mrs. Bardan's was the time set, because every Saturday at that time Mrs. Bardan was gone. That was when Annie would usually run over and visit Fritz.

Annie had special animal-rescuer clothes. First she pulled on long johns, then her faded jeans. For warmth. Then, for the first time, she wore her animal-rescuer blouse. It was cream-colored and buttoned in back. The collar had a ruffle, and on the front Annie had sewn on gold stars and crescent moons. The blouse had a matching gold ribbon which she tied in a bow. Then she put a pink wool vest over that and buttoned a blue lambswool sweater over everything. It was a heroic color, and she hoped David would notice how nice it looked with her red hair.

She brushed and brushed her hair until it sparkled. She spent a long time looking at herself in her round mirror over her dresser. Her eyes seemed to be extremely big that morning. She pouted as she looked at the dimple in her chin. She had no idea if she was pretty and was afraid she wasn't. Like most redheads, she had little freckles on her nose and very fair skin. The night before she had remembered to protect herself by rubbing moisturizing cream all over so as not to get a windburn.

It took so much thought, getting ready! But it was fun.

Carefully she lifted her belt out of the drawer. It was leather with a special brass buckle that said *Liberty*. She had won it at a fair. When she was finished, she compared herself to a ten-inch-high carved wooden figurine on her dresser. It was an antique that Aunt Rosie had given her on her tenth birthday. It was Miss Liberty with a crown on her head. She stood on a flowered globe that said *The United States of America*. Miss Liberty wore a long pink dress with a bodice that was cream-colored and had stars and crescent moons on it. It had given Annie the idea for her rescuer costume. Standing next to Miss Liberty on the globe, was a gray dog holding a book in his mouth.

I wonder if Fritz would like a book to read, Annie thought, giggling at the idea. She bent forward and kissed Miss Liberty for luck. Opening her door a crack, she peered out. Coffee smells! Her mother must be in the kitchen. The coast was clear upstairs, and she bounded up the steps to the third floor.

"April!" she murmured as she opened the door up there to the frigid attic.

The kitten was asleep near the door.

"Brrr . . . hi, April!" The kitten woke up and watched as Annie checked her bowls. "Oh boy, you haven't eaten anything. Aren't you hungry, baby kitty?" Annie stooped to pet her and held her up, close to her cheek. Finally April purred. "There!" Annie said, happy.

Annie looked around. There was almost nothing

to clean up. The newspapers were dry, the floor clean. Annie wasn't sure it was a good sign. April really needed the out-of-doors. Being cooped up alone couldn't be good for her. The kitten was pawing Annie's sweater.

"It's your big day!" Annie said. "You and Fritz are going to be roommates. I hope you like dogs." She stroked the tiny bony head with her finger. "We're going on a long trip to paradise."

The cat hung its head.

"Annie! What are you doing up there?" Mrs. Oberwager cried from the door that led to the third floor. "You're letting cold into the rest of the house." She was climbing the stairs. Annie could hear her footsteps.

"I'm just getting books!" Annie yelled, pushing April off her lap and jumping up. She closed the attic door behind her and ran to the stairs, meeting her mother halfway. "Do you know where my atlas is?" She made her eyes wide.

Her mother was shivering in a thin nightgown and robe. When Annie met her, she backed down, holding on to the railing.

"Oh, for your report?" she said.

"Yes!"

"You didn't find it? Let's look for it downstairs. Oh, you're wearing your beautiful blouse!" She closed the door at the bottom of the steps. "I wouldn't have put it in the attic, honey. The winter cold and summer heat aren't good for the binding."

Mrs. Oberwager found the big book in the sun-room, just where Annie knew it would be.

"Calm down, you look like there's a fire." Annie's mom laughed.

"I have a lot of work to do for this report. Can you make me pancakes, Mom?" All of a sudden she was coaxing. "That's the only thing that'll help."

"You're silly, that's why I like you. You going to see Fritz this morning?" Mrs. Oberwager asked as she led the way into the kitchen.

"I hope I'll have time to," Annie said, wincing. Her stomach growled at the thought of pancakes. She was hungry. At least that wasn't fake.

When Mrs. Oberwager was at the counter stirring things up, Annie put her arms around her mother's waist and gave her a hug, feeling the silkiness of her robe. She didn't want to think about lying to her sweet mother.

Five minutes before eight-thirty, Mr. Oberwager left for the foam rubber store. Mrs. Oberwager was spending the day doing errands and catching up on answering letters. Annie sat in front of a plateful of pancakes glistening with maple syrup. Six slices of crisp bacon surrounded the pancakes. Four of them she stuffed in her pockets. She was watching the clock, waiting for the phone to ring.

"Guess who's coming for supper?" Annie's mom asked.

"It's easy. Dr. Whitacre!"

"How'd you guess?"

"Because you asked him last week and the week before and the week before that and the week be—"

"I know! I like his Southern accent. He reminds me a little bit of my dad. And I know he misses his wife."

Mrs. Oberwager loved people. "I like the stories he tells. The one about flying squirrels was my favorite."

"Mine is the one about the time they thought the ear muffs were bats!"

They both laughed, and when the phone finally rang, it startled Annie so much she nearly threw her chair over in her haste to grab the receiver off the wall.

Mrs. Oberwager was saying, "I'll get it." But Annie beat her to it, waving at her mother, *it's for me,* until she heard the caller's voice clearly.

"Hello, Mrs. Oberwager?" the voice said tensely.

"Mrs. Oberwager?" again.

"Josie?"

"Yes," came the soft answer.

Annie felt her face flush. She was so surprised she couldn't think of what to say. Why was Josie calling?

Her mother was standing at the sink, rinsing dishes and looking at Annie with a little frown on her face. Her eyes were thoughtful. Annie's imagination was running away with her, but meekly she handed the phone to her mother.

Then she left the kitchen, ran upstairs, got her

pack, which was heavy with pet food, and dashed to the attic. She whipped the cat off the floor and stuffed her into the box she had prepared for her at top of the pack. The kitten made a little complaining sound but then was quiet. *Thank goodness,* Annie thought, on her way down again. From the foyer, with the front door open, she shouted. "Mom, I've got to meet Belinda! We're going to the library. If she calls, tell her I'm on my way. I'll call you this afternoon. Bye-bye."

EIGHT

☆

Annie, with April resting on top of the provisions in her pack—cans of dog food, a rope, a plastic water bowl, etc.—ran down the front sidewalk. She was feeling brave.

She walked carefully past Mrs. Bardan's house to see if she had gone. From the street it looked as though the garage door was open, but since it faced away from the street, she couldn't tell if the car was there. And then she saw something surprising.

Another car stood in the driveway. A spotless, new car with a Syracuse license plate and a bumper sticker advertising SunLand, the new recreational center.

Annie stole up Mrs. Bardan's little hill but far to the left of the cage. She was on the next neighbor's property now. Fritz was in the cage at the top of the rise and looking out at her. His tail wagged. She smiled but stayed away. Instead, she raced behind the garage, and peered through the window. She saw Mrs. Bardan's car. Her visitor must have kept the old witch from leaving at her usual time, Annie thought.

"Who's here, and is he going to mess us up?" she muttered to herself, feeling like socking the person.

While she waited, Annie set down her backpack and patted the crying kitten. "Shh!" she tried to warn the cat. Its mewing sounded like an alarm to her.

April was trembling. Annie murmured soothing, smoothing words. It was useless. She remembered that Belinda must be trying to reach her at home. After putting on the backpack again, Annie hurried toward her friend's house.

A door slammed, and Annie spun around. She was not far from Belinda's rabbit cage when she noticed a man in a suit coming out and walking toward the blue car. Quickly she ran behind Mrs. Bardan's garage and peered around the corner. She saw the man pause to look at the house and lawn. He noticed the cage—Annie saw him take a step toward it and frown. Was he the vet? Her heart stopped. Then he gave Fritz another quick glance and got into his car. He smiled at himself in the car mirror, then drove off.

Before Annie could move, Mrs. Bardan's door opened again, and she rushed out. As cold as it was she was carrying her coat. Her footsteps, usually plodding, were lighter. The coat was not her usual maroon one—it was a bright royal blue! She went to the car in the garage, started it up, and left. Fritz was not given as much as a glance.

Annie turned and raced toward Belinda's. This was it!

There was David cutting through the yard. And Belinda bursting through the back door. They were all ready to go.

Annie signaled. "She just left. I saw her go!"

"How long do you think we've got?" David asked, bundled in his layers of sweatshirts, with the gray one on top under a green down vest. He looked like a stuffed pepper. His eyes were shining, and his cheeks were pink from the nippy air.

"Oh, she'll be gone an hour anyway. Have you been running?" David's face was shiny with sweat.

"Sure have! When Belinda said you'd left before she even called, I thought we were in trouble," he said.

"Why'd you *do* that?" Belinda whined. "It confused me when your mom said you were already gone!"

"Sorry, Belinda! But Josie called her and I got so scared. See, yesterday, Josie found April, and I asked her not to tell. I was scared she had decided to tell Mom in spite of her promise. So I had to get April out before my mom could look in the attic. If she got mad at me, I was afraid she'd ground me."

David was walking toward Mrs. Bardan's house. "Can we get on with this rescue?" he asked.

Annie squeezed Belinda's hand, the cat meowed, and off they went for Fritz.

When the dog saw Annie, he whined. To her relief, he was still standing. He rambled toward the gate as Annie fiddled with the rusty hasp.

"There he is," she said in her softest voice as she opened the gate. She stroked Fritz's bent head.

"I see what you mean; he does look bad. Weak legs!" David said. He'd never seen Fritz before.

"He needs exercise is all." Annie scratched the dog's ears to pep him up. She felt a bit embarrassed by Fritz's ragged appearance, and Belinda giggled.

"Stop it!" Annie said, knowing Belinda had read her mind. "It's not funny, is it? Or else we'd be making jokes instead of saving him."

Annie felt very sure now of what they were doing. Fritz was waiting for what was in her hands. But first Annie pulled the rope out of her bag and handed it to Belinda, who attached it to Fritz's collar.

"We've got a surprise for you, Fritz," Annie murmured, holding out the bacon toward Fritz, then slowly backing out.

"He *is* nice!" David said. "We can massage his legs every day. That'll help him. Come on, boy!"

Belinda tugged on the rope to coax him out. As soon as Annie and the bacon went through the gate, so did Fritz.

"I didn't think he was going to do it!" Belinda shouted.

Fritz stepped stiffly. He looked at them as if he

were asking *What's going on here*? Everybody was encouraging him. "Come on, boy, that's the stuff!" David said.

"Guess he needs time to stretch and get going. After all, he's not a puppy," Annie said, scratching him and looking at his pretty eyes.

"Puppy! He's older than George Washington!" Belinda said.

David snickered but Annie, ignoring them, gave the treat to Fritz. "Close the gate, Belinda!" she said. "We don't want Old Snootface to notice Fritz is gone until we get out of town."

"Okay, okay!" they said.

Fritz loped down the drive. No cars passed on the street. Luck was with them. They were heading toward the country club golf course. Its far border was the city line of Syracuse. That was where the road was that led to the Oberwagers' farm. When the UPS truck went by, Annie waved at Bill, the driver.

"Don't wave, idiot!" Belinda shouted, very annoyed. "You're calling attention to us."

"He's my friend. If I asked him, he'd probably deliver us like a package to the secret cabin."

"All I can think is that he could be a witness in our trial for stealing Mrs. Bardan's dog." David moaned. "I'm hot in these stupid sweat shirts!"

"Would you like to carry April?" Annie offered, to cheer him. "I know she likes you better than my pack."

David walked behind her and unhooked the pack

to let April out. She nestled into his arms. "Hey! She's fatter now!"

"Wouldn't it be fun if we were all moving out to the cabin in the country?" Annie said.

"And we could live on our own like pioneers!" Belinda said, tugging Fritz by the rope.

Crossing Mohawk Road to the golf course, they all were singing. Annie, happiness bubbling inside her, bent down and ruffled Fritz's coat. His black hair rippled, and some strands stuck to her mitten. She dug her hands into his fur, wanting to pinch him— gently—to let him know that good things were happening to him at last.

"You're going to have a new home!" she said.

He turned and licked her hand.

"He understands. Huh!" Belinda said.

NINE

It took two hours to reach the country road. Fritz needed to rest at times on the way. Then April wiggled out of David's arms and ran off. They found her behind an old Dairy Queen stand on the road. Belinda was getting snippy, and David looked plain worried.

They all were upset that they had taken the dog from his cage, even though it was for a good reason. Annie promised herself that never, never would she steal anything—not even a sugar packet from a restaurant.

A huge yellow earthmover rumbled by them as they walked on the side of the old country road. Poor Fritz shied and pulled against the rope now held in Annie's grasp.

David, who was walking next to her, said, "You know you're going to have to spend a lot of time out here with these animals?"

"Don't be a worry wart! That'll be fun," she said, smiling at him. They walked in silence for a few minutes. Then Annie stopped and said, "I've got news for you guys. It's right . . . over . . . *there!*"

She pointed to a hill sticking up like the crown of a hat in a field of collapsed brown grass, bare bushes, and trees.

"Just behind it is the scout cabin!"

"Terrific! You can't see it from the road," David shouted. They crossed into the open field. "This is your land? We're not trespassing?" Nobody wanted to be doing anything else they considered wrong.

Annie nodded. "I told you. We own it, but a farmer oversees it."

Belinda smiled as she looked around. "The pets will be nice and warm here. The hill will protect the cabin from the wind."

"It's like a sentinel, the hill," David said.

"What's a sentinel?" Belinda giggled. "I know, nut! Don't tell me."

David knocked her with his elbow. They were hurrying up the hill now. Even old Fritz began to pick up his feet. His head jerked as he looked from side to side.

"New smells!" Annie said. "Look! He's coming alive."

She could stop pulling the rope. Fritz wanted to move. A congregation of crows meeting in a maple flew up and crossed the sky. A chipmunk ran through the grass. At the moo of a cow way off near the barn, Fritz's ears perked up.

David, looked behind him for the umpteenth time,

then yelled back at Annie. "I can't wait to get on the other side because I keep thinking that Mrs. Bardan or the police are going to catch up to us."

"Not a chance!" Annie said, sure of it now.

Belinda had disappeared over the hill. The cat was scrabbling against David's vest to get down. Suddenly Belinda appeared at the top again. She was jumping up and down and waving her arms joyfully.

"Oh, hurry, it's so pretty!"

April slithered down David and bounded across the grass.

"Go on, David, I've got Fritz!" Annie said.

He ran over the hilltop. Belinda disappeared with him.

"Now us, Fritz! Come on!" But the dog turned stubborn, and he plopped down to rest. "You crazy thing!" Annie yelled at him, laughing and pulling at the same time. Then she dragged him, and they went over the rise. She let go of the rope, dropped to the ground and rolled down the other side, propelling herself with arms and legs. She stopped at the bottom. "Yippee! Yippee! Yippeeeeeee!" she cried. Burrs were sticking to her clothes. Fritz licked her face.

"Stop nibbling, it tickles!"

David threw himself down next to Annie. "Wow!" he said. "This is neat." Annie couldn't even look at him, he made her feel so good. She was glad when he hopped up and went to the scarred wood door of the cabin.

"I'm going to hit it with my ax—okay?" David said, pulling one with a red handle out of his pack.

Your ax looks brand new," Annie said.

David grinned and nodded. "It is."

Bang, bang, bang he went, but the lock held until he socked it so hard it looked like he'd knock the door in. David's expression was so fierce when he did it that Annie was thrilled.

One window of the ancient cabin was bordered by faded, rough green shutters. They were entwined with thick ivy vines. The leaves were wrinkled and tarnished and climbed as high as the pointed brown roof. The roof swooped low, and Belinda could almost reach up and touch the wood shingles. Belinda hugged Annie and said that it was like finding Snow White's and the dwarfs' cottage.

"I've always wanted a secret clubhouse. Oh, Annie!"

David was pulling at the lock. Finally he yanked it off and heaved it over his head. "Come on, help me shove the door! It's stuck!"

It couldn't be budged more than halfway open, but they were able to squeeze through. Annie thought the smallness would keep the place warmer, and she was happy about it. She pulled Fritz's rope, and he followed. April was still outside, busy in the long grass.

The cabin consisted of one cozy square room with windows on all four sides. From the back window, they could see another hill rising behind them. A ladder led up to a loft, and David climbed up. Just then April walked in, a mouse in her teeth. Hunter's treasure.

"Oooh, gross!" Belinda said.

David, who was at the top of the ladder, jerked. Annie shrugged and said, "I think it's all right."

"Look at her, she's proud. She thinks we ought to stuff it for her like a trophy," David said.

When the dog sniffed it, Annie and Belinda decided to bury it under the front bushes. The kitten ran after them, and when they came back inside, April danced into the stone fireplace and pounced on dry leaves that had fallen down the chimney.

David called down from the loft, "They used to sleep here. There are cots. Like camp."

It *was* like a camp. Most of the furniture was made from logs. Inside the rough wooden cupboard, Annie found blue plates, yellow mugs, and drinking glasses.

"Does the water work?" Belinda turned the squeaky faucet. Rusty water trickled out. "We can clean!" She had thought to bring soap and rags in her pack. "Find a bucket, Annie!"

The water was on a pumping system, which had to be primed. Belinda pumped until the water ran clear. She filled a plastic bowl for Fritz and one for April. Then Annie dropped two big stones from outside into the bowls.

When Belinda and David looked at her strangely, Annie explained. "These are so if a mouse or bug falls in, it can climb out!" She patted Fritz.

"I never thought of that!"

"It's not my idea. My Aunt Rosie from New Mexico told me about a woman she knows who does that. Don't you like it?"

"I'm going to do it," David said. "It saves lives." He blew his nose.

Belinda, who began sweeping with a broom that was lying on the floor, told Annie to stop playing with Fritz and dust the windows. Annie didn't care about the windows, but she did it.

Soon the place began to look better. Annie was glad she had cleaned the windows. Everything looked much brighter. *If only we had a phone so I could call Mom like I promised,* she thought.

"Look at Fritz!" Belinda shouted from the tin sink.

He was circling the ragged rug on the floor. He sniffed it, disturbing the thick dust on it. He raised his head, looked around, sniffed again. Circled it over and over. Sniffed and circled. David shook his head. Slowly, like an old man easing himself into a rocker, Fritz settled down on the rug.

Sunlight fell across his back. He was in a bright circle that faded at the edges into shadow. All three had stopped to watch.

Annie smiled, feeling grateful for Belinda and David. They had helped her create a wonderful, safe home for animals.

TEN

During lunch, which David had brought, they discussed how they were going to care for the animals. "Riding a bike out here wouldn't take any time," David said. "Let's divide the feeding between us so we can keep up with it. I'm just real surprised the cat doesn't bother Fritz."

"She's a kitten, that's why they get along," Belinda said, balling up the waxed paper from her sandwich and sending it flying through the air. "Wheee, April!" The kitty chased it into the fireplace with her leaves.

"Wonder if we could bring Billy Bobblett here . . ." Belinda said.

"Him?" Annie said. "He's the dumbest kid in class."

But David surprised her by nodding his head at Belinda.

"Don't you know his folks are awful to him?" Belinda said. "The social workers have had to take him away from them, and he lives in a foster home."

"Abused." David said it so low Annie almost couldn't hear it.

She blushed. She hated having made that stupid remark. "What kind of things did they do?"

David just shrugged, and Belinda shook her head.

Annie folded her waxed paper neatly. She had never been nice or friendly to Billy and wondered if kids with brothers and sisters were naturally smarter about people than "only" kids were. "I hope he has some place as nice for him as this is for Fritz," she said, getting up. When she felt uncomfortable she liked to move.

David was lying with his head inside the fireplace. "It's dark, but you can see a little sky. After I clean the chimney someday, we'll build a fire here."

"Really!" Belinda got down next to him to look.

Annie was up on the kitchen counter dusting the cabinet's topmost shelf when her hand hit something. She pulled the object out. "Oh, look, a picture!"

David and Belinda came to see. In the old-fashioned frame was a photograph of a dozen boys in knickers and a tall, thin man. Sitting in front of them was a dog.

Belinda clapped her hands at the sight. "Look, isn't that a German shepherd?"

"Fritz is reincarnated!" David shouted.

Their dog looked up at his name. "He's come home to be with his old buddies," David said.

"Do you think they were really Boy Scouts?" Annie asked.

"No. Look, it says Shawnee Rangers, I think," David said, reading the faded print at the bottom of the photograph.

"Nineteen eighteen, wow!" Belinda said.

David sneezed again and again. His eyes watered, and Annie felt sorry for him.

Belinda pulled out a new pack of tissues and offered it to him. "The dust has to settle," she said sympathetically.

"I'm pretty allergic!" he said. Fritz wagged his tail when he sneezed again.

"I get hay fever in the autumn, and my nose turns red," Annie said, trying to lighten things, not wanting him to feel self-conscious.

"I'm okay!" He went outside for fresh air.

Belinda and Annie looked at each other.

"I like him just the way he is," Annie said, feeling she was brave enough to tell Belinda her special feelings about David.

"Me, too. Really," Belinda said.

The afternoon was rushing by. Annie was worried what would happen if her parents ever found out. Would they understand? Or would they find something terrible in what she had done? She never wanted to disappoint them.

Belinda tapped her arm. "I feel so good. We've saved Fritz, and April has a home!" She yawned. "Let's get stuff ready for them so we can leave." She called David, who had taken Fritz for a walk.

"He's all set!" David said when he came back in.

Annie had put the dog food cans on the counter, and David pulled out a Swiss Army knife. It contained all kinds of little tools. "At last I've got a good use for this!" There was a miniature can opener, and he opened two cans of food for the dog and one for the cat. They scraped the food into two of the Shawnee Rangers' blue bowls. April seemed hungry and rubbed against his pant leg. When Belinda put down the bowl for April, the kitten gobbled all but a teaspoon of food in her bowl. Annie put out another can for her.

"Isn't it lucky there's a pair of them? To keep each other company!" Belinda said.

"Except for the sign, that's it!" David said.

"What sign?" Annie said.

"We need an official sign. 'The Home for Animals' with Zack Gilligan's name under it. And then, 'Shawnee Rangers of America.'" David had Magic Markers and paper in his pack and took them out.

"But who's Zack?" Belinda asked.

"The guy in the picture—the leader. See?" David pointed to the photograph, which they had hung up on a nail near the door.

Sure enough, at the bottom of the picture were the words, *Shawnee Rangers, Zack Gilligan, leader.* When the sign was finished, David stuck it in the window.

Fritz was tied in such a way that he could go in or

out of the cabin. But from the moment they tied him, he stood and looked frightened.

"He knows we're leaving him. He's smart," Belinda said.

"You read his thoughts, Belinda!" Annie said.

"Yeah, I don't know how, but I—I can, can't I?"

They smiled at one another. They were very proud.

Belinda asked, "Don't you think the farm overseer will find him?"

"No. His house is all the way at the other end of the property. You have to drive down a different road to get there. And this part of the property's too hilly to farm. There's no reason for him to come back here." She hoped she sounded more confident than she felt.

"You'll be fine, Fritz!" David said, rubbing the dog's head. Then he asked the question nobody had dared to. "What are we going to do about Mrs. Bardan?"

Belinda, eyes wide, reached down and picked up April, who had curled up on her sneakers. Belinda stroked her fur.

Annie felt a flash of anger. "I didn't know we had to do anything. We don't want her to know where we've put him, that's all! Because if she did, she'd come and take him away. And then punish him for going off when it's not his fault. Even though she wants to gas him, she'll come and get him, I know it!" Her voice was getting higher, and she had to stop talking for a second and swallow. "I don't want to tell her anything! You promised me, David!"

"She'll think he's stolen and call the police!" David shouted in a panic.

"Oh, that's so nuts!"

"Why is it?" Belinda asked.

Annie had to stop and think.

"David's right, she will," Belinda said. "You're not seeing it the way it is, Annie. You're just dreaming everything's going to be all right because that's how you want it."

"And the police are going to come after us," David said.

"You're crazy; they don't know!"

"Annie! We only have to let her know he's safe and being taken care of. After all, *think!* She fed him at least," David said.

"Yeah, she does deserve to know," Belinda said.

"I told you my secret and now you're . . . you're . . ." Annie couldn't believe it. She felt as if she were drowning. "Why can't you understand?"

Belinda jumped up, dumping April off her lap, and gave Annie a shake. "You're being a jerk. What are you yelling at us for? We're trying to keep you and us out of trouble." She burst into tears.

"We don't have to do anything about Mrs. Bardan!"

Belinda was wiping her eyes and sniffing. David looked desperate.

"Annie . . ." He dragged out the word, "Annie . . . come on. You don't have to be mad. We're not going to tell anyone about your place. Don't we want to keep it safe, too? You know that, huh? It's our secret too, now."

His words stopped Annie's drowning feeling. She tried not to be panicky, to listen, and most of all to think. But nothing was going to ruin the home for animals, she thought fiercely. "You know . . . some people steal animals. Like those rare tropical birds poachers sell. But we didn't steal—we *rescued*. If babies or children or—Billy Bobblet, for instance, is mistreated, they need help from somebody. Just like Fritz did," she said.

Now they were listening.

"*Someone* has to rescue a poor old dog who's helpless," Annie said.

David folded his hands across his chest. "She'll *think* we *stole* her property."

Annie looked straight at him. "What does it matter?"

Taking in a huge breath, he shrugged. "It just does."

Annie stroked Fritz's head. "The only thing I can think of is to—maybe pay her? For her piece of property?"

"Pay her for *what*?" Belinda said, coming out of her cloud. The tears were gone.

But David was nodding his head. "Hey, you know, you're right! We can write her a letter. We'll say we wanted to have Fritz and that we'll take very good care of him. Then we'll put in some money and sign the letter—"

"Sign it what?" shouted Belinda. "'Love, Annie, David, and Belinda'?"

"Anonymous. The Animal Rescuer Society. Zack Gilligan," Annie said. "It's great! But I've spent all my allowance on the food. I could find maybe eight dollars from my birthday money." She hated to give that woman good money, especially since she was going to have to keep buying pet food. But if it meant they owned Fritz, she would do it.

David said he could give five dollars, and Belinda was shamed into contributing, too. Her promised two dollars made a total, a nice total, of fifteen dollars.

"For a nearly dead dog," she muttered.

It was late. They all petted Fritz. Annie told him that she would be back first thing in the morning. He seemed to take it fine. "I love you," she whispered when the others weren't looking and hugged April tightly and said the same thing to her.

Then David showed April once more the ashes and crumpled leaves in the fireplace. "Your kitty litter, in case you didn't want to go outside. No pooping in the house!" he said firmly as they all stepped through the narrow opening of the door to leave.

Belinda and Annie giggled at his words all the way to the road.

"If you're going to be an animal's best friend, you gotta tell 'em like it is!" he snapped.

Belinda rolled her eyes at Annie and whispered, "I think he'd better learn to talk *dog* and *cat* if he wants it to work!"

ELEVEN

☆

At the Oberwager home, the lights were already lit, glowing in the late afternoon semidarkness. Annie saw that her dad's car was in the driveway. He was already home from the store. Worried, Annie ran her hand along the car's smooth side as she walked on the driveway to the walk leading to the front door. Was feeling so anxious a reaction to being so brave that morning?

Just let me be able to save Fritz, she prayed before turning the doorknob slowly and quietly. *Let it work out! Please!*

There was a good smell in the house. Lasagna, she thought. When the door opened, the warmth of the house and the thick red carpet underfoot welcomed her. Her breath streamed out in a long sigh. She had done it; Fritz was safe in the country!

She listened, heard voices in the kitchen, and tried to catch the words. Suddenly there was a third voice. Her heart sank. Josie!

Annie crept to the kitchen door. She heard

Josefina say in a loud voice over Dad's, "Oh, I've got to talk this over with the kids."

Talk what over? Annie wondered.

Annie's dad laughed when Josefina said, "It may be that I'm a mite *afraid,* did you think of that?"

Then Mrs. Oberwager said, "Oh, phooey! You'll love it; think of the kids!" and Josie said, "We-el." She sounded happy!

"Have you *ever* flown?" Mr. Oberwager said.

Flown? wondered Annie.

"Well . . . not in these times . . . hijackings, crashes, and all."

Her father laughed gently. He must have known Josie hated admitting she hadn't yet had an airplane ride. Annie knew she never got to travel.

"Well, talk it over, Josefina! We'd love to give you the tickets, wouldn't we, Miriam?" Mr. Oberwager said, and Annie's mother agreed.

What in the world is this about? Bundled in her warm clothes, Annie began to perspire. She was hungry, too. The dinner smelled delicious. And she was going crazy wondering what was going on with Josie.

Josefina said after a long pause, "I've thought that if He wanted me or the children to fly, God would have put wings on us."

Mrs. Oberwager giggled. "Well, if that's right, He'd have had to give sailors boat-bottoms, wouldn't He?"

Annie slapped her hand across her mouth to stifle a laugh. Her mom was funny!

"Well," Josefina said, sounding relaxed again, "guess I won't get to tell Annie myself so when she comes in, please give her my big news."

Annie opened the door and burst in on them. "What? What, Josie, what do you want to tell me?"

"Were you listening at the door?" Dad said, stepping back when Josefina jumped up and grabbed Annie.

"Child, wait'll you hear what's going on!"

Mom yelled, "Annie, you're back. Oh, good! I was getting worried." She sounded thrilled, not irritated.

"Big news! It came in a letter in a long white envelope." Josefina held it up. "Thought I was being sued, Annie! So I had to call up and ask your mama to read me what it said. Then I had to wait *all* day to find out. I couldn't find someone to stay with the little ones, and my big kids stayed overnight at their cousins'."

Josefina straightened up to her full height and then said, in a thrilled voice, "Josie is going to New York. With the children. To be on TV! This letter from Ms. Julie Kielson says Mr. Martin Sawyer, *the* Marty Sawyer, wants me on the *Bright Sunday Morning Show* for the Easter program. In two weeks! Me and the kids are supposed to sing and do our birdsong chorus for them. On *TV*!"

Annie screamed.

"And I got you Oberwagers to thank for it. Didn't

you get me to send that record we did in church? Didn't you write the letter and put in the newspaper clippings on us—God's Songbirds? Wait'll my kids hear this!"

It was a miracle all the way around. Annie's parents were so excited about Josefina's news that neither of them said a word about how long Annie had been gone.

Annie gazed at Josie happily. What a wonderful thing for a hardworking lady! With no husband to help her, Josie was raising four children. The TV station was going to pay them a thousand dollars. "More money than I've ever seen!" she said. "But I love the Lord more than money!" she added quickly.

Annie said, "This is a great world, Dad, isn't it?" She put her arms around him.

"Yes, it is, sweet face," he said and gave her a big hug.

"Wait'll I get my stuff off, Josie. We can have a quick reading lesson before you go home," Annie said.

"Haven't got time for that, hon."

"No? Just a quickie! Give me the letter." Annie's eyes ran down the page when Josefina passed it to her. "See, what's this word?" she said finding the one she wanted and pointing.

Josefina looked and frowned. "That's a capital *E* and a little *a-s-t-e-r.* Ummm, what . . . is it *Easter*?"

"What do you think?"

"Its spelling sure sounds like it."

"You're reading, Josie! Honest and true. Really reading."

The grown-up Oberwagers smiled at each other.

"I'm going to pop the buttons off my sweater if I hear any more good things. If I get too vain, *you*'ll be cleaning this house! So you all better be careful! Lemme run." Josefina kissed Annie goodbye and whispered to her not to worry about the cat. "I didn't say a word," she said. Annie had no chance to tell Josie that the kitten had a home.

Mr. Oberwager insisted Josie accept a ride home instead of taking the bus.

"Only if I can ride in the back like you're my chauffeur. That's how good I feel." She clapped her violet hat on her dark hair and flashed a smile.

"It's okay by me!" Mr. Oberwager said.

"Next week I'll probably hit the littery!" Josie said.

Annie and her mother ran to the front window to see if Josefina was truly going to ride in the back of the Cadillac. Sure enough, Mr. Oberwager opened the back door for her, and she got in. At the sight, Annie and her mother hugged each other.

Little did they know then that Josefina was on her way to fame and fortune in the music world. One day she would hire her own limousine. So practicing having a chauffeur now was right in line with what life in all its mystery and surprise—"some good, some bad," as Josefina said so often—was going to bring her.

TWELVE

☆

They were having lasagna because it was Dr. Whitacre's favorite. Annie rushed upstairs to get ready for supper. She washed her face and hands and changed out of her animal-rescuer outfit. Then she laid out the money to give to David for Mrs. Bardan tomorrow.

As she hung up her animal-rescue blouse and belt, she thought it was odd nobody except her mother had mentioned them. *Are they kind of funny looking?*

When she went downstairs, she yawned and said, "I'm sleepy, Mom!" She took her place at the table across from their guest.

"All that studying in the library wore you out," Mrs. Oberwager said sweetly. "Did it go all right? Annie has a big paper," she explained to Dr. Whitacre. Annie quickly nodded. Her father said grace about all creatures feasting one day in paradise, and they started eating.

Dr. Whitacre was a handsome old Southerner

with silver hair. He treated Annie like nobody else did, as if she were a *fine lady*.

"All my patients were ladies," he said. He had attended the births of 12,000 babies. "And when I treated my patients as fine ladies, I noticed they took better care of themselves."

"When did you know you wanted to be a doctor?" Annie asked between mouthfuls of lasagna.

"Oh, when I was a mere boy. My sister Elsie died in childbirth," he said. "Then when I was nine, my parents made the most money in their dry goods store one Saturday that they had ever made. And no banks were open to take the money. So my papa stored it in the desk drawer downstairs, which made Mama quite uneasy. She made him lock the screen door before retiring to bed. In those days we were accustomed to leaving doors unlocked.

"Mama forgot that our cousin Drew was staying with us for the weekend and was out when they went to bed. Drew was courting a Windsor girl, and when he came home, he found himself locked out."

"So what happened?" Annie said. She was trying to find the connection between this long story and his becoming a doctor. "How does this—" she started to ask.

Dr. Whitacre gave her a stern look. If anybody interrupted in the middle of a story he was apt to forget the rest. Her mom was signaling silently to remind her. Annie bit her lip. Fortunately, he continued.

"Drew began to pound and rattle the door. The racket woke up my folks. Mama screamed, 'They're after our money!' and fainted dead away on the floor. When I heard her cry it woke *me* up. My papa had picked up a fireplace poker to arm himself and rushed downstairs to discover poor lovesick, skinny Drew at the door. Papa was so shocked he about hit Drew over the head. But he caught himself in time, thank the good Lord. He turned to run upstairs to tell Mama, so he could relieve her mind about the money's safety.

"When he burst into the bedroom, he saw I had come in, lifted Mama into my arms and was staggering with her toward the bed. A kind of amazing strength had filled me. Beds were high then; you should have seen me! Only nine years old. Fortunately Papa got there in time to assist me in these labors. . . ." Dr. Whitacre caught his breath and swallowed water from his crystal goblet.

"Mama was still unconscious. We didn't have a doctor in our little town, and they had to send all the way to Colerain, North Carolina, to get one."

"How far?" Annie said.

"About twelve or fifteen miles. The doctor, when he arrived, was so welcome! I remember my heart turned over from plain gratitude—I was that thankful! Dr. Garnet, that was his name, said my mama was purely exhausted. Having revived her with smelling salts, he prescribed complete bed rest and gentle foods, easy to digest.

" 'Son', he said to me—people often used that appelation for young boys—'I want you to be her nurse. I see how responsible and sensible you are.' "

"Well, that's what I did. Gave her sips of water and coaxed her to eat until she was herself once again and the smiles lit up her face. It took about a week."

"Didn't you have to go to school while she was sick?"

"No, ma'am, Annie! Nothing was as important as Mama. I stayed right by her side. And I always remembered how respectfully Papa and everybody else treated Dr. Garnet. That's when I decided to become a doctor, and that's all there was to it!"

"I love that story!" Annie said.

She ate the rest of the meal in silence, thinking the story over. She chose bits of it for herself. She imagined one day telling about the beginning of her career as an animal rescuer. She pictured herself as a famous old lady. She pictured herself having a TV program on how to be your pet's best friend. She saw David and herself on a huge ranch with horses, goats, llamas, bobcats, deer, rabbits, killer geese, dogs—mutts and sleek pedigreed ones and lots of cats.

They were eating strawberries zabaglione when something unusual for a Saturday night happened. The doorbell rang. Its sound brought the blood rushing to Annie's head.

She closed her eyes, hoping against all hope that it

would be skinny, lovesick Drew from Dr. Whitacre's story.

Instead, when her father went to the door and opened it, everybody in the dining room heard the very serious voices of two police officers, a man and a woman.

"We're looking for a Miss Ann Oberwager," the man said.

THIRTEEN

"A Mrs. Bardan has filed a complaint. She's waiting down at police headquarters this very moment to hear what we can find out from questioning a Miss Ann Oberwager at this address. Is she in, please?" the officer who had introduced himself as Lieutenant Galt asked Mr. Oberwager.

"Annie! My Annie?" he said in an utterly amazed voice. "What could you want with her?" He was standing in the open door, letting the heat of the house stream out into the night.

Annie, her mother, and Dr. Whitacre had left the table when the voices filled the quiet house. They had moved to the living room, where they could see the hall and front door. Annie was in front, her mother behind her saying, "Annie?" Dr. Whitacre, who had a linen napkin still tucked into his shirt like a bib, was beside Mrs. Oberwager.

Annie's father turned and noticed them. He looked back at the police officers.

"Come in," he said hesitantly, closing the door behind them. His face had flushed pink. "There's Annie. This is Lieutenant Galt and Lieutenant Roybal."

Annie took a numbed step toward them. She fervently wished that, like Dr. Whitacre's mama, she could faint dead away.

The officers looked at each other. "This is your only Ann?" Lieutenant Galt asked.

Mr. Oberwager nodded.

Lieutenant Roybal, a hefty, good-looking woman, put up her hands. "She's a kid!"

"Well. What is it, officers?" Mrs. Oberwager asked, moving in front of Annie and looking ready to take charge. Only Annie may have heard the telltale tremble in her mother's voice. She was scared.

Lieutenant Roybal took a step toward the living room where the group stood. "You are Ann Oberwager?" she asked. "Mrs. Bardan, your neighbor, is missing her German shepherd dog, Fritz."

Annie felt heat rush to her cheeks. She took a gulp of air and heard her mother gasp. Her father took a step forward toward Annie. Dr. Whitacre cleared his throat. Everyone was looking at her.

Silence. A horrible silence.

"The dog was discovered gone late this afternoon."

So she didn't notice until then, Annie thought. The silence continued. She didn't know what to say.

"Mrs. Bardan has reported it to us. Can you help us locate the whereabouts of the missing dog, little girl?" Lieutenant Galt finally said.

She clenched her teeth together until they hurt. Everyone was looking at her, and everyone seemed to expect that she did know something. There was no way she could pretend innocence, as much as she longed to say, "I've never seen or heard of this dog, Fritz!" She would have choked on those words like a bone.

"Annie!" her father said sharply. He was probably embarrassed by her delay in answering the police officers. He did not like rudeness.

Her heart pounded.

"Can you help us out, Ann?" Lieutenant Galt repeated, coaxingly now. "Mrs. Bardan said you often visit Fritz. If you just tell us what you know . . ."

Annie solemnly shook her head. By accident he'd given her the word she needed: *can.* "No sir, I *cannot.* I've made a promise I can't break."

The eyes looking at her widened. Especially the woman police officer.

"Annie, what is this?" Mrs. Oberwager asked.

"Mom, it's a rescue." Annie tried to control the pleading sound in her voice. She needed most of all for her mother to understand for once, without knowing everything. Her mom, who loved animals, too, just like she did. Suddenly Mrs. Oberwager looked down at her shoes. *She got it!* Annie thought. She, too, was disturbed by Mrs. Bardan's treatment of Fritz.

"Well, since you can't explain this to us for some

reason or other . . ." Lt. Galt began, irritation replacing the softness and ease he'd shown at the beginning. Annie noticed a red splotch under his eye.

"The only reason is, I promised," Annie said firmly.

Dr. Whitacre coughed, obviously uncomfortable with her behavior.

". . . we'll have to go down to the station where Mrs. Bardan, who is very upset, is waiting." Lieutenant Galt thundered over her voice. He was angry. Lieutenant Roybal whispered something to him. Annie trembled.

Mr. Oberwager lifted his hand and scratched a spot inside the crisp collar of his shirt. He was plainly confused. "Okay. Guess we have to go."

Without any fuss, the family got their coats. They apologized to Dr. Whitacre for the interrupted dinner, but he shook his head.

"For a well-brought-up youngster to say she wouldn't answer the police . . . my, my! This must be very serious. I will accompany you. Perhaps I can be some help or comfort, Douglas?" Dr. Whitacre said.

Annie looked at him. "Dr. Whitacre, it's just that I can't answer anything until I talk to—some people."

He nodded. "I see."

She surely hoped he could.

"Annie," her father said, as he got into the back of the police car with her (Mrs. Oberwager was riding with Dr. Whitacre), "try to see the world without an enemy, okay?"

She couldn't answer. And didn't want to! It was taking all her strength to keep her heart from pounding right out of her chest.

FOURTEEN

☆

The architect who designed the Shawnee Precinct Station must have loved flying more than anything else in the world. The building had a high ceiling and looked as if it was rising into the sky. The room where victims of crime and people accused of crime came was a soaring room with tall windows.

As soon as Annie walked through the carved wooden door, she caught sight of Mrs. Bardan. She was one of a number of people sitting on wooden chairs that were lined up against one wall. The Oberwagers walked toward her with their police escort and Dr. Whitacre. Here in this tall space, Annie thought, Mrs. Bardan didn't look quite as frightening as at her home.

When Lieutenant Galt and Lieutenant Roybal brought Annie and her family over to her, two young men sitting there moved off, freeing chairs.

Mrs. Bardan, her new royal blue coat hugged around her, stared silently and accusingly at Annie. Lieutenant Galt asked her to identify which one was Ann Oberwager.

She nodded toward Annie.

"This is the person you meant?" he asked.

Mrs. Bardan nodded when he touched Annie's shoulder. Her eyes were strained and tired.

"Hello, Mrs. Bardan," Mr. Oberwager said politely. "Can't you say hello, Annie?"

She said hello. Mrs. Oberwager sat down one chair apart from Mrs. Bardan, after the police directed her to do it. Annie's mother's lips were pressed together. She wasn't able to greet Mrs. Bardan the way her husband did.

"Annie did not answer our questions about your missing dog, but seemed to know about it. Would you care to question her yourself, ma'am?" Lieutenant Galt asked.

Mrs. Bardan nodded. Annie steeled herself.

"What do you know about my dog?" she said fiercely, her eyes suddenly flashing. She was furious.

"I know—I—"

"Annie, please," her dad warned.

She gave her answer to him. "All I know is that Fritz was very, very sad," Annie whispered.

"What? What? Speak up, dear!" Lieutenant Roybal said, putting a warm hand on Annie's shoulder. "Sad? Why?"

"He was abused . . . caged all the time . . . half-crippled. And he was never petted since he was hit by a car."

Lieutenant Roybal's round brown eyes looked

into Annie's. She wanted the truth, and Annie was giving it to her.

"I know that Mrs. Bardan is going to put him to sleep. She called the shelter to ask if they'd do it for free!" She nearly choked on the word *free* and looked at her mother, whose eyes opened wide. She guessed exactly what had happened. Annie knew it.

"And so?" Lieutenant Roybal asked softly. Lieutenant Galt, in the chair next to Mr. Oberwager, was slowly nodding his head.

"I have known Fritz all my life. He's Mrs. Bardan's dog but he is my friend."

"Oh! Bet you don't have a dog of your own," Lieutenant Roybal said kindly.

"I don't but it's all right. We can't have any pets. My dad's allergic. But . . ." She didn't know whether to actually confess she and her friends had rescued the dog. She certainly was not going to mention their names. *Imagine David being right about what would happen.* She sighed.

"So what happened when you found this out?" Lieutenant Galt prompted. "Where is Fritz?"

Mrs. Bardan's mouth twitched. At least she hadn't denied anything. Annie felt her own face burning. She was in a trap for sure. Dr. Whitacre harrumphed, and Annie said, "He's safe now. That's all I can say. Nobody can put him to sleep."

Mrs. Bardan shouted, "You bring my dog back! Where is he? Officers, can't you help?"

Annie, feeling dizzy by now, shook her head no. The officers remained silent.

"Fritz is my property. You'd *better* tell me where he is."

"He's not property!" Annie cried back.

Somebody gasped. She didn't see who. "He's a living creature."

"You've stolen my dog."

"I didn't. He was rescued, and he's happy, too!" Annie, who'd been fighting tears, suddenly felt them stinging her cheeks.

"Annie!" her dad said, looking as hurt as she had ever seen him. "You can't take this lady's dog. You've got to tell us where he is."

"I promised, Dad. I can't break a promise. I can't!"

"Whew!" he said, rubbing his hand clear over his shiny head down to his neck. "Annie, oh Annie!"

After that all conversation stopped. Lieutenant Roybal then asked Mrs. Bardan if she could please talk to her privately. The two women went into an office to the left of the tall desk where suspects were booked. Annie's parents sat on each side of her and explained how she had to give back the dog. Annie said she couldn't. She felt sad and scared now because even her mom seemed to think she had to give Fritz back.

Lieutenant Roybal returned a few minutes later, without Mrs. Bardan. Her expression was almost cheerful. Annie looked away from her and up at a large clock. It was 8:47. Annie hoped Fritz was lying fast asleep on his rug. She prayed April was nestled by his side. Only by thinking of them safe and content could she stay brave.

"Annie," Lieutenant Roybal was saying, "can you trust me enough to go with me now to talk to Mrs. Bardan? She's calmed down and I promise you I have no tricks up my sleeve." She smiled encouragingly.

It was the last thing Annie wanted to do, but her dad's look made her quickly obedient.

"Remember what I said now," he whispered as she stood up and followed Lieutenant Roybal. "No enemies!"

"Help me!" Annie prayed, for suddenly she knew she was powerless to save Fritz by herself. Help was needed. She was sure of that.

FIFTEEN

The three of them met in Lieutenant Bertha Roybal's office. It was tiny, with a desk and three chairs squeezed into a windowless space. There was a telephone on the desk, a notebook, files, and some family photographs. Three were school pictures of children.

Mrs. Bardan and Annie were seated side by side, so at least they didn't have to look at each other. They could look into the quiet, open face of Lieutenant Roybal. She told Annie that she had a ten-year-old daughter, Sara Rosa, who could keep secrets, too. She loved animals, especially dogs. She told her things about Sara Rosa that Annie didn't think she needed to know, yet Lieutenant Roybal's voice was kind and soothing. There was nothing tricky or bossy about her. Annie guessed she could trust Lieutenant Roybal. When Mrs. Bardan said in a much quieter voice that she was tired and could she please go home to rest, Lieutenant Roybal said, "Of course, Mrs. Bardan!" in as kind a voice as she spoke to Annie.

"But first, can you please tell Annie your plans? You can see she has been so worried for these months since your Fritz was injured—"

"I just want my dog back!" Mrs. Bardan flared up, but then she sighed.

"Of course you do," Lieutenant Roybal said kindly. "But we have a misunderstanding here. Don't you see that Ann is worried about Fritz? And only you can relieve her worry. She doesn't know, does she, that you yourself haven't been well—that you've been really sick?"

Mrs. Bardan nodded at that. Annie was surprised to hear that the old woman had been ill. She wondered what was the matter with her.

Lieutenant Roybal looked from one to the other. "Neither of you *has* to go away completely unhappy and unsatisfied tonight, if you just realize that both of you have a key to help Fritz and yourselves."

"What is it?" Annie asked, mystified.

Mrs. Bardan pursed her lips. She probably didn't want to use the key, whatever it was.

Lieutenant Roybal was looking directly at Mrs. Bardan now, but smiling at her, too. "Mrs. Bardan?" It was a prompting voice, the one Annie's teachers used when she was daydreaming sometimes.

"Should I tell her I'm moving?" Mrs. Bardan asked the officer, who nodded. "I'm moving, Annie, to a condominium in Florida."

"Oh, I didn't know that. Why?" Annie asked.

"Her health," Bertha Roybal put in.

What's wrong with her? Annie wondered again.

"I can't take a dog to the condominium. They don't allow it. He's too old for anybody to want, so I have to put him to sleep."

"That's not true. I want him; he's wonderful!"

"Nobody wants an old dog!" she said decisively.

Lieutenant Roybal looked at her with a smile. "Are you sure of that, Mrs. Bardan? Here's Annie!"

The woman looked as if she hadn't heard. "Knowing I'd have to do this was hard on me . . . with everything else." She sounded so tired, even weak. Mrs. Bardan!

Annie was getting a different picture of Old Snootface. She felt her cheeks get burning hot.

"And . . ." Lieutenant Roybal prompted Mrs. Bardan again.

"Well . . . *and* I only need Fritz as a watchdog a little longer. Until April thirtieth, when the movers come."

"Good! Oh, good! You told her!" Bertha Roybal laughed with relief.

Mrs. Bardan is moving away! Annie thought. It felt so strange to know that.

Suddenly Mrs. Bardan shivered and started to cough. She put her hand to her neck. She looked as though coughing hurt.

Annie said, "Mrs. Bardan, what's the matter? I didn't know you were sick."

"Now you're beginning to understand, honey," Lieutenant Roybal said.

Mrs. Bardan said, "I have a tumor." She touched her neck again. "Here, it presses near my ear. It's like an earache, but it doesn't go away."

"Oh!" Annie thought it must be terrible when pain didn't go away. "I think you'll get better!" she said, hoping.

Mrs. Bardan stood up; she looked confused.

Bertha Roybal said, "It's all right, you can go, Mrs. Bardan. I know you're ready for some rest."

Mrs. Bardan nodded. "In Florida where it's warm, I think my ear will feel better, too."

Annie thought that was good news.

"Once I've worked things out with Annie, your good neighbor, I expect we'll be bringing your dog home tomorrow."

Annie was confused. Mrs. Bardan turned and said, "Good night, Annie," in a voice unlike a witch's.

Annie was now alone with Lieutenant Roybal, who looked down at her desk, thinking. Annie waited for the policewoman to say something. What would she say? Lieutenant Roybal cleared her throat.

"Evidently Mrs. Bardan does have some feelings for her dog, Annie, don't you think so?" she said at last.

Annie had to nod her head.

"But because of the situation, she was burying those feelings, right?"

"I guess so."

"Think she wants to put Fritz to sleep?"

"Maybe not . . ."

Bertha Roybal smiled.

"I'm not going to give her a chance to, either!" Annie said stubbornly.

Lieutenant Roybal didn't stop smiling. "Of course not. What you've done saved his life. You were brave."

Annie was amazed.

"You made the lady think. She found out how she feels when she was hiding it even from herself."

Annie shrugged. What good would it do?

"But now you've got a new problem, Ann. Mrs. Bardan needs her dog until April thirtieth, and afterward you have to come up with a place that both you and your parents say Fritz can live. Now your folks are in on it, too."

"She said I could have him?"

Lieutenant Roybal said, "Not yet, anyway, but I know you've got a chance!"

Annie rubbed her cheeks with her hands. It was hard to believe this was happening.

Lieutenant Roybal stood up. Annie did, too.

"No, dear, I'm going to go out. You can stay and use the phone to call the people . . . well, I don't know who you promised, but Mrs. Bardan needs her dog, Annie. She doesn't feel safe in the house without him nearby. So you use the phone and see if you can't decide what to do now. . . ."

She opened the door and closed it behind her. Annie was left alone.

SIXTEEN

☆

No one answered the phone at David's. Belinda wasn't allowed to get calls after eight. Annie sat there, staring into space. Finally she put her head down on her arms and rested. If only her heart would stop its terrible pounding.

"I'm not shocked," Mrs. Oberwager was whispering. "Somehow I'm not surprised."

Annie stirred at the sound of her mother's voice.

"But the police station's no place to sleep. Both Dad and I want you to come home."

Her mother kissed the back of Annie's neck.

Annie raised her head. "David didn't answer."

"I know."

Annie realized with surprise that she had given away part of the secret by mentioning his name. "I can't do anything until I reach him or Belinda," she said, deciding to trust her mom.

"Let's go home, Annie; we can work it out there, okay?"

Dr. Whitacre had driven Mr. Oberwager home earlier to get his own car. Annie got into the car with her folks after explaining to Lieutenant Roybal she would try to call her "people" tomorrow morning first thing. Mrs. Oberwager explained to her husband, who was very quiet on the drive home. She had figured out everything except where the dog was.

In the early morning, Annie went first to David's and then to Belinda's. They heard the news at David's rocky hill where the quarters were buried. A lavender crocus was blooming there.

"What's your news?" Belinda said. Annie told it.

David didn't say anything when it turned out he was right about Mrs. Bardan's calling the police. Belinda had a funny expression on her face, but she made no mention of it either. They dug up the quarters and sat quietly thinking. No one smiled, but there was a sense of relief.

Belinda said, "I'm so glad I don't have to give my money to Mrs. Bardan."

David said, "I'm going to check on Fritz and April while you and Belinda stop at Mrs. Bardan's. All you say to her is that she can have Fritz back if she promises to let us take care of him after April thirtieth. How's that?" David said.

They nodded.

"Otherwise she'll have to get him over my dead body!"

"And over mine!" Belinda said.

"Mine, too!" Annie said, so grateful she could have jumped up and touched the sky. "Yippee!"

Mrs. Bardan promised.

David came back to say April and Fritz were doing fine. April seemed to know the cabin was home. Fritz had wagged his tail. That afternoon Mr. Oberwager picked Fritz up and delivered him to Mrs. Bardan. Annie couldn't do it. She cried at the thought of Fritz being back in the cage.

On April twenty-eighth, a Sunday, Fritz returned to the Oberwager farm from Mrs. Bardan's house to live for the rest of his life. Annie had called the man who cared for the farm, and he said he would keep an eye out for her new pets. But Mr. Oberwager said since Annie had taken this on, she was responsible. He was upset about what she had done, but told her he knew she was trying to do what was right.

"It isn't always easy to know exactly what is right. The rules and laws often help us to know. But sometimes we follow our own inspiration, and it goes against our laws. In those cases we must take the consequences, no matter what." He was fond of quoting Martin Luther. "It's not always possible for people to know the good, the will of God. They sometimes have to act without being sure. 'Sin bravely,' Martin Luther said, 'but hold Faith even more bravely.' You did, Annie, and I don't like it, but I don't think you did wrong."

Every day Belinda, David, and Annie rode their bikes out to feed and play with April and Fritz. Both were in very good health now. Fritz had a glossy coat and a vet had checked his hip. Annie had paid for it with her savings and a loan from her father. Fritz jumped up whenever they came. He could fetch and run. He could beg for crackers.

"This dog is poor Fritz no more!" Belinda said.

Lieutenant Roybal and her daughter Sara Rosa came to see the animals. "I wanted you to meet Annie!" she said to shy Sara Rosa, who held the cat but didn't say much.

"Bless you, Annie!" Lieutenant Roybal said, to Annie's amazement.

On May fifteenth, Annie called Belinda at nine-thirty A.M. "Belinda, I've got news for you . . ." she began.

"Oh, no you don't," Belinda interrupted. "David already called and told me. You *like* each other, and now you're not going to talk about anything else!" She was so mad.

"That's not true! I just wanted to tell you a Mrs. Wagner has moved into Bardan's house and she has four dogs!"

"You're kidding!"

"No, and she'll let us see them!"

"Really?"

"She's wonderful! Meet you there in five minutes!" Annie sighed. *Guess I might as well call David, too.* Her heart went thumpety-thump, but she was getting used to that.

ABOUT THE AUTHOR

BARBARA BEASLEY MURPHY writes for children and young adults. She is the author of *Annie at the Ranch* and the coauthor of *Ace Hits the Big Time* and *Ace Hits Rock Bottom. Ace Hits the Big Time* was selected as an ALA Best Book for Young Adults and was made into a CBS "Schoolbreak Special." She was a fellow in writing for children at the Breadloaf Writers Conference, and won the Christopher Award for *The New York Kid's Book* of which she was coeditor and contributor. Her other books include *One Another,* and *The Antelope Dancer,* to be published in 1992, the 500th anniversary of Columbus's arrival in America. It is the story of a contemporary Pueblo boy who lives in two worlds, the ancient Indian one and the New World created with the coming of Columbus.

A member of the Authors Guild and PEN, she was sponsored by PEN's The American Right to Read and the Authors Guild to address the banning of *No Place to Run,* a book for young adults.

She and her husband Bill, a painter, live in Santa Fe, not too far from San Ildefonso Pueblo, where *The Antelope Dancer* takes place and the horse farm where *Annie at the Ranch* is set.

THE SADDLE CLUB

A blue-ribbon series by Bonnie Bryant

Stevie, Carole and Lisa are all very different, but they *love* horses! The three girls are best friends at Pine Hollow Stables, where they ride and care for all kinds of horses. Come to Pine Hollow and get ready for all the fun and adventure that comes with being 13!

☐ 15594-6 HORSE CRAZY #1 ....$2.99
☐ 15611-X HORSE SHY #2 ....$2.99
☐ 15626-8 HORSE SENSE #3 ....$2.99
☐ 15637-3 HORSE POWER #4 ....$2.99
☐ 15703-5 TRAIL MATES #5 ....$2.99
☐ 15728-0 DUDE RANCH #6 ....$2.99
☐ 15754-X HORSE PLAY #7 ....$2.99
☐ 15769-8 HORSE SHOW #8 ....$2.99
☐ 15780-9 HOOF BEAT #9 ....$2.99
☐ 15790-6 RIDING CAMP #10 ....$2.95
☐ 15805-8 HORSE WISE #11 ....$2.95
☐ 15821-X RODEO RIDER BOOK #12 ....$2.95
☐ 15832-5 STARLIGHT CHRISTMAS #13 ....$2.95
☐ 15847-3 SEA HORSE #14 ....$2.95
☐ 15862-7 TEAM WORK #15 ....$2.95
☐ 15882-1 HORSE GAMES #16.................................$2.99
☐ 15937-2 HORSENAPPED! #17 ....$2.99

Watch for other SADDLE CLUB books all year. More great reading—and riding to come!